"Stop ⸺⸺⸺⸺⸺⸺⸺ ⸺ing to escape his embracing arms.

Her heart was racing and she fought the treacherous urge to relax against him, to surrender to her body's yearning for his touch. But she couldn't succumb to him again, she thought frantically. Pushing at his chest with renewed determination, she warned him, "If you don't let me go immediately, I'll—I'll call all the kids into the kitchen!"

Greg laughed. "Now there's a threat! All of them stampeding in, demanding food or drink or popsicles at the top of their powerful little lungs." He released her and held up his hands. "See? You're free. So, please, don't sic the, er, little darlings on me!'

Maggie sighed. The man really was irresistible. . . .

WHAT ARE *LOVESWEPT* ROMANCES?

They are stories of true romance and touching emotion. We believe those two very important ingredients are constants in our highly sensual and very believable stories in the *LOVESWEPT* line. Our goal is to give you, the reader, stories of consistently high quality that may sometimes make you laugh, sometimes make you cry, but are always fresh and creative and contain many delightful surprises within their pages.

Most romance fans read an enormous number of books. Those they truly love, they keep. Others may be traded with friends and soon forgotten. We hope that each *LOVESWEPT* romance will be a treasure—a "keeper." We will always try to publish

LOVE STORIES YOU'LL NEVER FORGET
BY AUTHORS YOU'LL ALWAYS REMEMBER

The Editors

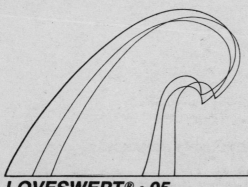

LOVESWEPT® • 95

Barbara Boswell
Darling Obstacles

BANTAM BOOKS
TORONTO • NEW YORK • LONDON • SYDNEY • AUCKLAND

DARLING OBSTACLES
A Bantam Book / June 1985

ISBN 0-553-21707-0

Published simultaneously in the United States and Canada

---

*Bantam Books are published by Bantam Books, Inc. Its
trademark, consisting of the words "Bantam Books" and
the portrayal of a rooster, is Registered in U.S. Patent and
Trademark Office and in other countries. Marca Registrada.
Bantam Books, Inc., 666 Fifth Avenue, New York, New
York 10103.*

PRINTED IN THE UNITED STATES OF AMERICA

O   0 9 8 7 6 5 4 3 2 1

One

To Mary Magdalene May, Greg Wilder fell into the same category as Alan Alda or Tom Selleck or Robert Redford. All were appealing masculine gods—admirable, handsome, interesting—and unquestionably, totally, inaccessible. There were some differences, of course. Greg Wilder wasn't a famous actor, although as an acclaimed neuro-surgeon he was a celebrity of sorts in the planned community of Woodland, Maryland, where they both lived. And they were on speaking terms: He called her Maggie and she called him Dr. Wilder. He was the father of her son Kevin's friend Joshua, and she was the sometime baby-sitter for three of the Wilder children.

Maggie wasn't surprised when Dr. Wilder arrived two and a half hours late to pick up the children on that warm Friday evening in early October. Doctors' schedules were often erratic and unpredictable and he had been late before. She had simply stretched the tuna casserole by adding more noodles and fed Josh, Wendy, and Max along with her own three kids—Kristin, Kevin, and Kari. Josh had asked for seconds, Wendy had eaten a few small bites, and Max had thrown down his fork, pronounced the dinner "yucky looking," and demanded a peanut butter and jelly sandwich. Maggie had good-naturedly complied; her own kids had had their definite food preferences at age four too.

It was eight-thirty when Dr. Wilder finally arrived. The children were gathered in the small living room watching the annual presentation of *The Wizard of Oz* on television. Maggie's ironing board was set up in the corner of the room and she occasionally glanced at the TV as she ironed. She was wearing cutoff jeans and a sleeveless yellow blouse in concession to the unseasonably high fall temperature. It had reached eighty degrees that afternoon and the little frame duplex would be a long time cooling down. Her dark auburn hair was pulled up high on her head in a ponytail that just skimmed the nape of her neck. Although her brother often teasingly told her that she looked more like twelve-year-old Kristin's sister than like her mother, Maggie thought that she looked every one of her thirty-two years. She certainly felt it.

The doorbell rang twice in quick succession. Not one of the children looked away from the screen, although Kristin did call out, "Someone's ringing the doorbell, Mom."

Maggie unplugged the iron and went to the door. Greg Wilder stood on the step, resplendent in a black tuxedo and frilled white shirt. He was quite tall, at least two or three inches over six feet, and had the hard, disciplined body of an athlete. He somehow managed to make his fancy suit look ruggedly masculine, Maggie noted wryly, in spite of the white frills. His hair was light brown, streaked blond by the sun, and he wore it short and parted to the side. Maggie knew that the Wilders owned a sailboat and a high-powered speedboat and spent many of the summer weekends on the water. All the Wilder children had that same sunstreaked blond-brown hair.

"Hello, Maggie. Sorry I'm late." Greg Wilder smiled at her, his blue eyes crinkling at the corners. His eyes were the most unusual color of blue that Maggie had ever seen—light and clear, the color of aquamarines—and they were surrounded by a fringe of long, thick, dark lashes. His younger daughter Wendy had his eyes—large and wide-set and absolutely striking. Maggie's heart began to beat a little bit faster. It often did in Greg Wilder's presence.

"I was held up at the hospital," he continued, "and then had to rush home and change and pick up Francine." He inclined his head toward his impressive burgundy Cadillac parked along the curb. Maggie squinted into the darkness and saw a shadowy figure in the front seat of the car. His date for the evening, Francine. She would be gorgeous, Maggie knew. All Greg's dates were.

"Are the kids ready to go?" he asked.

She nodded with a smile. "Yes, they're watching television. I'll call them." He made a slight move forward and Maggie, who was holding the screen door ajar, quickly closed it. "I'll send them out right away, Dr. Wilder," she said.

Greg Wilder remained outside on the doorstep. He always waited on the doorstep for his children, except in bad weather, when he would return to his car to wait. Maggie had never invited him inside. Their conversations were always, inevitably, held in the doorway.

"Your daddy is here," Maggie announced to the group in front of the TV set. The Wilder children—nine-year-old Joshua, seven-year-old Wendy, and four-year-old Max—seemed not to have heard her. They didn't move a muscle or glance away from the screen.

"Max, Wendy, Josh!" Maggie made her tone as cheerful and bright as the voice of the Good Witch of the North. "Daddy is waiting to take you home."

"I wanna watch the show," Max said, tightening his arm around his bedraggled teddy bear.

Maggie caught Kristin's eye and sent her a silent appeal for reinforcement. Sometimes Max listened to Kristin when he wouldn't obey anyone else. Kristin picked up her cue. "You can watch the movie at home, Max. On your great *big* TV."

"No!" Max said, scowling fiercely. "I'll miss the good parts driving home. Teddy and me are staying here."

Kristin shrugged and turned her attention back to the program. The ball was back in Maggie's court. "Max, honey, I'm sorry but you can't stay here," she said firmly. He looked so cute, sitting cross-legged on the floor clutching his bear. Maggie had an admitted soft spot for him and keeping her tone firm wasn't easy. But she couldn't keep the child; his father was outside waiting to take him home. "Your daddy is waiting for you, Max. He has to go out tonight and—"

"Go out?" Joshua turned his head at that. "On a date, you mean?"

"Well . . . I guess so," Maggie hedged. She *knew* so, but the thunderous expression on Joshua's face kept her from making a completely affirmative reply. Coward, she accused herself.

"He goes out too much!" Joshua burst out with sudden ferocity. "Every Friday and Saturday night that he isn't on call at the hospital. And then he gets in late and is grouchy the next morning and misses my soccer games—"

"He doesn't always miss them, Josh," Kevin interrupted. "He was there last week, remember?"

Maggie gave Kevin a fond smile. Her nine-year-old diplomat. But Josh wasn't prepared to be reasonable. "We lost last week, so that doesn't count!"

"Be quiet! I can't hear the TV," complained six-year-old Kari. "Why don't you go home now?"

Definitely not a diplomat, thought Maggie with a sigh, and wondered how to extricate the Wilders gracefully from her living room. She knew from experience how stubborn and irascible they could be. Josh and Max could be, she mentally corrected herself. Wendy was quiet and passive and almost too docile. Sometimes it unnerved her, the way the little girl never expressed preferences or choices or any emotion at all. Wendy stood up now, her small face impassive as usual, and stared from Maggie to her brothers with those big beautiful aquamarine eyes of hers.

"Wendy is all ready to go," Maggie said hopefully. "Come on, boys, let's see you two race to the car."

Maggie congratulated herself on her clever psychological strategy when Josh jumped to his feet and headed for the door. "I'll beat you, stupid!" he called over his shoulder to Max.

"Bad move, Mom," Kristin said dryly, eyeing Max. The little boy's face was contorted with fury and he stretched himself out on the floor and began to kick his feet and scream "I'm not stupid! I'm not going home!" over and over again at the top of his lungs.

Kristin, Kevin, and Kari watched him, far more fascinated with the tantrum than with *The Wizard of Oz* at this point. Maggie suppressed a groan. None of her children had ever had temper tantrums, not even during the "terrible twos." And though Josh sometimes made reference to his little brother's tantrums, Max had never had one while in Maggie's care. Now he appeared to be making up for lost time. Momentarily nonplussed, Maggie simply stood and watched along with her children.

"Daddy says Max is too old to have tantrums," Wendy said in a half-whisper. Maggie was inclined to agree, but that didn't solve the problem of what to do with the furious, howling, and kicking child.

"Mom, do you want me to ask Dr. Wilder to come in and get Max?" asked Kevin.

Maggie glanced around the small, crowded living room, littered with cups and doll clothes and GI Joe paraphernalia. Her ironing was in two big plastic baskets in the middle of the room. She visualized Greg Wilder in all his masculine elegance wading through the mess and shuddered. For some stupid reason—misplaced pride perhaps—she was loathe to have him see her looking tired and disheveled in the thoroughly untidy room. If and when Greg Wilder ever did come into her house, she wanted everything to be in perfect order—herself, the house, the children, everything. Right now the house was a wreck and she didn't look much better. Maggie grimaced. The contrast between her and his beautiful date sitting in the front seat of the air-conditioned Cadillac would be excruciating. She quickly pushed the thought aside.

Max was continuing to shriek and Kevin took matters into his own hands. "I'll get Dr. Wilder," he said.

"No, Kevin," Maggie said quickly, nervously. "Let's give it a few more minutes."

She knelt beside the screaming child and laid her hand on his head. He was perspiring and his small face was wet with tears. What must it be like to be four years old, she wondered, the youngest of four children, with an extremely busy father and no mother? To have spent the last two years, half of your life, being shunted between baby-sitters and pre-schools, every day a different place with different people, and no routine or structure to depend upon? Maggie's heart suddenly wrenched for this small bundle of protesting fury.

She remembered Max's mother well. Alicia Wilder had been an attractive brown-eyed blonde who was always elegantly dressed and groomed to perfection. Maggie had met her four years earlier when Kevin and Joshua were enrolled in the same morning kindergarten class. Woodland was a planned community, halfway between Baltimore and Washington, D.C., with neighborhoods for all income groups. Its public schools were excellent and used by all the children in town. "That's what is wonderful about Woodland," Maggie had once heard Alicia Wilder say to another mother. "The children have an opportunity to mix with other children from all walks of life. Greg and I briefly considered sending our kids to a private school, but we decided that Woodland schools would definitely broaden their outlook."

In fact, young Joshua Wilder's outlook had been so broadened that he had chosen Kevin May for his best friend. The relationship between Joshua, from upper class Woodland Heights, with its elegant stone and stucco homes on acres of wooded land, and Kevin, from low-income Woodland Courts, with its frame duplexes and adjoining communal yards, could have served as a perfect example of Woodland's liberal social promises. Alicia Wilder frequently told Maggie how much she liked Kevin and how glad she was that he was Joshua's friend. But Maggie couldn't help noticing that while Kevin was often invited to the Wilders' to play, Joshua was seldom allowed to play at the Mays'. She suspected that Alicia Wilder didn't care for her son to be involved in the rough-and-tumble neighborhood of Woodland Courts. It was only after his mother's death a little over two years ago that Josh had begun to spend most of his free time at the Mays'.

Poor little Max, Maggie thought. The image of the lovely Alicia faded from her mind as she stroked the child's hair. "Max, I know you're tired and upset and very angry." She spoke in calm, soothing tones. "And you must feel that you—"

"What's all this about, Max?" The deep masculine voice seemed to fill the room. Max momentarily stopped screeching to glance up. His father was standing on the threshold of the living room, his arms folded across his chest, his sandy brows arched, and his lips drawn together in a tight line. He looked very big, very authoritative, and very angry. Maggie scrambled to her feet, feeling oddly breathless. Greg hadn't waited to be asked inside. He had entered on his own initiative.

"Mommy," Kari whispered as she carefully moved behind her mother. Kari, usually so feisty and funny, was timid around men, a fact of which Maggie was becoming increasingly aware. Unlike Kristin, who'd known a loving father until the age of six, Kari had never lived with a man in the house. John May had died just one week after the birth of his youngest child.

Greg Wilder crossed the room to stand over his small son. "We're going home, Max." His voice brooked no argument. At least it didn't to Maggie, but Max merely turned his head and resumed his tantrum.

"That's enough, Max," Dr. Wilder spoke in tones that Maggie guessed would have set the hospital staff scurrying to do his bidding. Max Wilder completely ignored him.

Maggie watched a dark red flush stain the doctor's neck and spread upward to his face. "He could stay here tonight, Dr. Wilder," she suggested quickly. "There's an extra bed in Kevin's room. He has bunk beds."

"If Max gets to stay here, then so do I!" Joshua was back and he glowered belligerently at his father. In his ire, the boy was a smaller image of the man, except for his eyes which were a light brown. Josh had his mother's eyes.

"You are all going home," Greg Wilder said through clenched teeth. "Joshua, Wendy, go to the car! Right now!" Wendy snatched Max's teddy bear and scooted out of the room. Josh followed, his face sullen. Greg leaned down and picked Max up in his arms. To the Mays' collective, fascinated horror, the child proceeded to punch, kick, and scratch his father, his screams of rage never abating. Greg Wilder strode from the room, carrying Max while attempting to fend off his blows. Maggie and her children followed them out to the car.

Joshua and Wendy were already in the back seat. Francine, a striking brunette in a low-cut red cocktail dress, was scowling in the front seat. Greg stuffed the shrieking Max into the back. "Maggie, I'm sorry about this," he said, turning to her. He appeared totally harassed. He reached into his coat pocket and withdrew a gold monogrammed money clip. Maggie watched all three of her children's jaws drop as he produced the thick roll of bills. She was sorely tempted to turn them away from the sight.

Greg peeled off a twenty dollar bill and handed it to her. "I hope this is enough, Maggie. I know you've had them since they got out of school at three-thirty."

"They had dinner here too," Kevin piped up.

Maggie felt her cheeks turn scarlet. Greg handed her another ten and she drew back, refusing to take it. "That's too much, Dr. Wilder. You—"

There was another shriek from the car, but this time it came from Francine. Max was in the front seat, attacking her. "Good Lord!" Greg muttered. He raced to the car and flung open the door to attempt to remove Max from his victim. Francine's hair was mussed and there were scratches on her slender neck and slim bare arms. Greg succeeded in prying Max loose, but not before he'd sunk his little teeth into the woman's hand. She gave an outraged howl of pain. The doctor roared at his son and began to spank him, all the while dodging the boy's flailing fists and feet.

Max continued to wail at the top of his lungs. Several interested neighbors converged upon the scene to observe and comment on the situation. Life in Woodland Courts was like living in the proverbial glass house; everyone felt free to mind everyone else's business. Joshua hopped out of the car and joined the group.

"What happened?" Kevin asked him. "Why did Max attack your dad's girlfriend?"

"She told Max if he didn't behave himself, she was going to throw his teddy bear in the Potomac River," said Josh.

The neighbors gasped in shocked disapproval. "That is no way to talk to a child," reproved Mrs. Jenkins, a grandmother of eight who occupied the other half of the Mays' duplex. For the past five years she had stayed with the May children at night while Maggie worked the eleven to seven shift at the desk of a major airline in nearby Baltimore.

"That awful lady should be ashamed of herself!" Kari exclaimed indignantly, her hands on her hips.

"Does your father know what she said to Max?"

Maggie wondered aloud. She agreed with Mrs. Jenkins and Kari. It had been a cruel remark to make to a child and the beauteous Francine *should* be ashamed of herself.

"No, he doesn't know," Josh replied cheerfully. "And Max got her really good! She's bleeding!"

"Maggie!" Max was sobbing now, his howls of fury changing to those of a hurt, frightened child. His father stopped spanking him and dumped him into the back seat of the car. Without glancing at the interested little crowd of spectators, Greg Wilder climbed into his car, slammed the door, and fiercely gunned the engine. The big Cadillac lurched forward, then tore away in a burst of speed.

"Hey, he forgot Josh," Kari said, giggling. The neighbors laughed. Someone made a remark about big shots with fancy cars and fast women and neglected children.

"Let's go inside," Maggie said quickly, and shepherded the four children into her half of the duplex.

"You can stay here tonight, Josh," she told the boy. "You can borrow a pair of Kevin's pajamas and we have an extra toothbrush."

"Come on, Josh, let's finish our Lego fort," Kevin said. The two boys raced up the narrow staircase to Kevin's bedroom.

"Can we watch Dorothy now, Mommy? It's just about the time she should be in the witch's castle," Kari said, taking her mother's hand.

"She knows the whole movie by heart," observed Kristin with big sisterly indulgence.

"So do I," Maggie said, smiling. "Let's go in and watch Dorothy outsmart the witch." She guided her daughters into the living room where the television and her ironing awaited them.

Ten minutes later the doorbell sounded again. "Do you think it's Dr. Wilder, Mom?" Kristin asked apprehensively.

Kari looked alarmed. "Don't answer it!"

Her daughters' anxiety disturbed Maggie.

Recently on a TV talk show she had heard a psychologist explain the results of a study conducted on the daughters of widowed mothers. The effects of their fathers' absence began in childhood, when the little girls tended to be nervous or fearful around men, and extended into the teenage years, when the girls acted wary and shy around boys their own age. According to the eminent psychologist's latest book, the girls' inability to relate to men could hamper them in forming lasting attachments with the opposite sex.

Maggie tended to disregard most of what she heard from the so-called experts, but this particular study had struck a nerve. Was it happening to Kari and Kris? she thought, frowning. Had the lack of a father or a father figure begun to instill a fear of men into her daughters?

"He'll hit Josh, Mommy!" wailed Kari.

"There is no reason to be afraid of Dr. Wilder," Maggie said firmly. "He doesn't go around indiscriminately hitting children. He was very angry tonight and Max was misbehaving and—"

The doorbell rang again and she hurried to answer it. The girls remained where they were. Greg Wilder was at the door. The debonair, self-confident man who had appeared earlier was gone, replaced by an obviously embarrassed, flustered parent.

"Dr. Wilder, please let Joshua spend the night here," Maggie said quickly. Her voice quavered and, much to her dismay, she sounded as anxious as Kristin and Kari.

Greg looked down into her upturned, pleading green eyes and heaved a heavy sigh. What a hell of a day this had turned out to be! he thought. He'd been in surgery since seven A.M. emerging between operations only to talk to the patients' families. The most grueling case, both physically and emotionally, had been a six-hour operation to remove a malignant brain tumor from a twenty-year-old college student. It had been impossible to remove it all and he'd felt like crying along with the family when he'd told them the grim prognosis. His meeting with the residents on his service had been overly long and he had stopped for a final check on his patients, thus landing him in the thick of Baltimore's weekend rush hour traffic.

When he had finally arrived home he had found his fourteen-year-old daughter Paula ready to leave to spend the night at a girlfriend's house. She hadn't been pleased when he'd reminded her that she was supposed to baby-sit for her sister and brothers that night. When he had left the house, Paula had been in her room sulking, having told him that he was the meanest and most unreasonable father in the world for making her change her plans.

Going to the dinner-dance at the Riverview Country Club with Francine Gallier was probably the last thing he felt like doing tonight, but she had invited him three weeks ago and he had accepted, and he felt obligated to go. He had tried to generate some enthusiasm by mentally listing her attributes. She was beautiful, sensual, exciting—good company and good in bed. And he needed to relax, to socialize, to be with a woman. The demands of his profession, his concern about the children . . . He had to have some outlet, didn't he?

Was he rationalizing because he was feeling guilty about leaving the children for yet another evening? he had wondered as he'd driven back to Maggie's to pick up Josh. He had been totally unprepared for the dreadful scene with Max. Max's temper tantrums were becoming an increasing source of concern. When he'd heard the unceasing howls from Maggie's living room he had charged inside to intervene. Now he was back on the doorstep, with Maggie holding the screen door only slightly ajar. Some things never change, he thought, grimacing.

"Max and Wendy were crying in the back seat," he said, "and Francine was smoldering in the front when I realized that I'd left without Josh." Greg heaved another sigh. "Damn. I—I feel terrible about spanking Max. Alicia would have been horrified. She didn't believe in corporal punishment of any kind and until recently"—his shoulders sagged—"neither did I."

Maggie watched him, listened, unsure of what to say. Their doorstep conversations were always light and pleasant and laced with the more humorous aspects of childrearing. They smiled a lot and never alluded to any problems. But Greg wasn't smiling now; he looked tired and discouraged. She wasn't sure if he was addressing her or merely voicing his thoughts aloud. A great wave of sympathy washed over her.

She felt sorry for the man, she realized with some surprise. She'd never really considered how complicated his life actually was; he always seemed so cool and in total control. For the first time she viewed his life from another angle. His profession was a difficult and demanding one, and having total responsibility for four children would have to increase the pressure on him to appalling levels. Why, it was no wonder he needed to go out, to socialize, to be with a beautiful woman like Francine. But when he tried to do it, he was sabotaged by his kids!

Greg noticed how Maggie was clutching the door as she stared at him. "And now here *you* are," he said, "staring at me as if I'm a confirmed proponent of child abuse." He was totally disheartened. "You needn't plead to keep Josh here to protect him from the wrath of his monster father."

"I was thinking no such thing," Maggie said swiftly. "I—I was thinking how very tired you look, Dr. Wilder."

Her unexpected remark took Greg by surprise and he stared down at her. There was no condemnation in her eyes, only compassion and warm concern. He had seen her look that way at the children, his and her own, but never at him. And she hadn't made some flippant joke either; she'd answered him seriously. He couldn't remember the last time they'd had a serious conversation. Their doorstep chats were invariably light and humorous and superficial. "I am tired, Maggie." He ran his hand through his hair, tousling it. He felt a sudden urge to sit down and talk to her seriously, to share his depression and the helplessness he felt about the sad future of his young patient, to tell her how worried he was about his children and how guilty he felt about failing to meet their needs. She would understand, he knew it instinctively.

But there was no time to talk. Francine was waiting for him and they were already late for the dance. And how could he sit down and talk to Maggie when she never let him inside her house? There wasn't a whole lot to say when relegated to a doorstep. Greg sighed again and condensed all his feelings into a weary, "It's been a . . . rough day all around."

"I understand," Maggie said soothingly.

He gazed into her warm green eyes and was astonished by his longing for her understanding, for her comfort. He felt compelled to deny that longing. "You couldn't understand!" he burst out. "You've never experienced the frustration and the regret and the guilt I've felt in dealing with my kids. You're the perfect mother, struggling to get by on your husband's death benefits and your baby-sitting fees and working that miserable night job, but never slighting your kids. You've been baby-sitting for my children for the past two years and four months, and I've watched you, Maggie. You're patient and kind and selfless, the type of parent every kid deserves to have. Your kids are happy and well-adjusted. *You* never lose your temper or yell at your kids or—or hit them!"

Maggie had to laugh at the image his words evoked. "You make me sound awesomely saintly, a regular Mother Machree. And though I'm tempted to let you go on believing that I have a halo over my head, I wouldn't dare. One of my kids might tell you about the time they tracked mud into the kitchen ten seconds after I'd finished washing and waxing the floor. I chased them around the yard with a mop, screeching like a banshee."

Back to humor again, Greg thought. He tried to smile, but the result resembled a bleak grimace. Maggie used jokes to shut him out, he realized with a sudden flash of insight. And it was just as effective as keeping him outside her house, on her doorstep.

Maggie waited expectantly for Greg to laugh at her little joke. She wanted to lighten his mood, to make him smile. But he didn't. He looked even more glum. She dropped all attempts at humor and said honestly, "Actually, there have been countless times when I've felt tired or depressed or angry and have taken out my feelings on my children. I know all about guilt and regret. I'm sure *all* parents experience the same feelings you mentioned at one time or another, Dr. Wilder. It goes with the territory. And I think single parents feel them doubly hard."

Greg shrugged and shifted uncomfortably. What was the matter with him? Right now he felt an incredible longing for her to stroke his hair and soothe him, much in the same way he'd seen her comfort Max. He was half-afraid he might totally disgrace himself and blurt out his need. "You're very understanding . . ." His voice was stiff and controlled. "I don't usually carry on this way . . ."

Maggie was certain he regretted his impulsive outburst and wondered if she'd been presumptuous, offering an experienced doctor her own unscientific opinions. But he looked so drained and discouraged; she wanted to comfort him somehow. She felt an almost overwhelming urge to put her arms around him and smooth away those lines of exhaustion and worry from his face. Thoroughly disconcerted by her feelings, she sought to banish them by mocking herself. Greg Wilder certainly didn't need *her* to comfort him! He undoubtedly had women standing in line to do the job. One of them was in his car right now.

Donning her protective emotional camouflage, Maggie slipped back into the role she knew best, the comfortable maternal role. "Dr. Wilder, why don't you let Max and Wendy spend the night here with us?" Her voice was soft, pleasantly melodious, a mother's voice. "The two little girls can sleep in the girls' bedroom and I'll move Kristin into my room. Kari would be absolutely thrilled to have Wendy and—"

"You can't tell me that any of them will be thrilled to have Max," Greg interrupted wryly.

Maggie grinned. "Oh, Kristin and I both get a kick out of Max. And the other kids enjoy him, too, though they might not want to admit it. I have a cot I can set up in Kevin's room and all three boys can sleep in there tonight."

Greg considered her offer. It would certainly simplify things if the three younger children stayed here. Paula could spend the night with her friend and stop sulking, and after the dance he could go to Francine's apartment and spend the entire night there. Usually, he had to stumble out of bed when he most wanted to sleep, get dressed, and leave his date's apartment to drive home because he didn't dare leave the children alone all night. His decision was made. "Thank you, Maggie. The kids can stay here. I really appreciate it." Now why didn't the idea of a child-free, passion-filled evening with Francine excite him? he wondered. He should be feeling as blissfully free as a teenager with the family car and no curfew. But he didn't. He felt flat . . . and oddly lonely. He reached for his money clip. "Let me pay you in advance."

Maggie shook her head. "Oh, no, Dr. Wilder. This doesn't count as baby-sitting. Tonight my kids are having their good friends over to spend the night with them." A slight breeze ruffled her hair and she smoothed her bangs back in place with her left hand.

She was pretty, Greg mused, watching her. He'd always thought so. Lovely complexion, high cheekbones, cute upturned nose, and soft, well-shaped mouth. Why, even in those old clothes she was wearing she . . .

Maggie was aware that he was staring at her and

lowered her eyes, embarrassed. He had never looked so long and so hard at her. Lord, she knew she looked bad tonight, but she obviously looked even worse than she thought. The contrast between her and the elegant Francine clearly had stunned him. He couldn't seem to take his eyes off her. Maggie made a mental note to pitch her ancient clothes in the trash tonight.

She knew he was staring at her, Greg realized as he saw her lower her eyes. And she was uncomfortable about it. Her rigid posture and clenched hands were proof of that. He immediately sought to put her at ease, saying the first thing that came into his head. "I see you still wear your wedding ring." He glanced down at his own ringless hand. "I, uh, stopped wearing mine a year ago." It had begun to feel strange, dating while wearing a wedding ring. When he'd finally accepted the fact that he was no longer a married man, he had removed his ring. But Maggie hadn't. Did that mean she still considered herself married to her dead husband? The notion disturbed him.

Maggie was staring at the gold band on her finger and was about to comment when a sharp, impatient voice called "Greg!" from the car. Both Greg and Maggie glanced toward the sound to see Francine leaning out the window. "Greg!" she called again. "We're late enough as it is. By the time we get these kids back to your house and—"

Greg stopped listening and looked at Maggie, his expression a combination of embarrassment and irritation. Suppose it were Maggie in his car, waiting for him? He couldn't imagine her behaving as peevishly as Francine. "Greg!" Francine's voice rose imperiously.

"*These* kids happen to be *my* kids, Francine," Greg said as he strode to the car, his tone as sharp as hers. "And they're spending the night here." Wendy and Max were out of the car in a flash, running toward Maggie. The old brown teddy bear was tucked under Max's arm and Greg felt a sudden, sick pang of remorse. What kind of father was he anyway? Whacking a four-year-old, then dumping his kids for the night so he could wine, dine, and bed a bitch like Francine Gallier?

Maggie had picked Max up, and his arms and legs were wrapped around her like a little monkey's. She was smiling as she carried him into her house, her one arm draped casually around Wendy's shoulders. Greg felt a crazy urge to follow them into the house. Not that he would ever make it inside, he told himself. He watched them enter the small frame duplex, noting bleakly that neither the children nor Maggie had cast a backward glance or called good-bye to him.

When Maggie answered the ring of the doorbell seven minutes later, she was astonished to find Greg Wilder at her door again.

He gave her a rather sheepish smile. "I'm sorry to disturb you again, Maggie, but may I use your telephone?" He half-expected her to refuse and point out the phone booth at the corner of the street. But she paused only a moment before replying, "Of course. This way, Dr. Wilder."

She led him into the kitchen and pointed to the white wall phone, immensely relieved that the dinner dishes were done and put away. She asked no questions, but he gave her an explanation anyway. "I have to call Paula. She was going to baby-sit for the kids tonight, but since they're going to be here, she'll be able to go to her friend's house and stay overnight. She'll be overjoyed." And he would no longer be the world's meanest dad.

Maggie nodded. Paula Wilder was very pretty and led an active social life, according to an admiring Kristin who was in the seventh grade at Woodland Junior High where Paula was in the ninth.

A sharp blast from a car horn shattered the silence and Greg frowned. "Francine thought I should phone Paula from the club, but it's nearly a forty minute drive from here and . . ." His voice trailed off. He couldn't explain his urge, his *need,* to come back. Nor could he explain the surge of pure pleasure that had rushed through him when Maggie had greeted him at the door. And now he was inside her house, invited. Well, almost.

He dialed the number, listened, then replaced the receiver. "The line's busy. Paula talking to her friends, naturally." But he didn't care, he admitted to himself. He was in no hurry to leave Maggie's small kitchen. No hurry at all.

The horn blared again and Greg's fingers tightened around the telephone receiver. Maggie saw his knuckles whiten, his jaw clench, and his aquamarine eyes grow cold as ice. "I'll be happy to call Paula for you, Dr. Wilder," she said quickly. "You have a long drive ahead of you and I know you're anxious to leave." At least Francine was. Another sharp, staccato blast of the horn made Maggie jump. She pictured the gorgeous, furious Francine sitting in the car and summoning her man with the horn, and she marveled at the woman's confidence. The expression on Dr. Wilder's face was making *her* nervous, and she had nothing to do with its cause.

Greg ignored the imperious demand of his date and strolled to the refrigerator, which was covered with children's drawings and school papers. "All A's," he remarked. "I guess the bad papers don't get put up, do they?"

Maggie was tempted to tell him that her children did not bring home any bad papers; they received nothing but A's and gold stars. She was enormously proud of their school success, but she didn't want to sound like a braggart. She just smiled noncommittally and said nothing.

"I remember Josh telling us that Kevin was the smartest boy in his class." Greg examined a math test of Kevin's, which boasted a smiling face sticker and a big red A+ at the top. "That was a couple of years ago, before Alicia . . ." He turned his attention to Kevin's social studies test, which bore a blue A+ and a SUPER written in capital letters by the teacher. "Kevin seems to be doing very well so far in fourth grade." Maggie nodded. "I wish some of his habits would rub off on Josh," Greg added wryly. "Alicia used to say that Josh was an underachiever. His teacher last year claimed that he wasn't any kind of achiever at all. I'm hoping he'll do better this year."

"Mmm," Maggie murmured. Apparently Greg didn't know how poorly Josh was doing in school this year. The first report cards hadn't been sent home yet, but from what she'd heard from Kevin and from Josh himself, Dr. Wilder wasn't going to be very pleased with his son's progress—or lack of it.

Greg dialed his number again and hung up at the busy signal. The car horn sounded again, a long, angry blare. He ignored it. Maggie had a smattering of freckles across the bridge of her nose, he observed. They looked cute. Wholesome and appealing. And he liked being in her kitchen. It was warm and homey, unlike the sterility of the barely used kitchen in his house.

The horn again. "Please let me make the call for you, Dr. Wilder," Maggie said. Her offer was more like a plea. He was staring at her again. He had the most beautiful eyes she'd ever seen. And when he looked at her she felt . . . she wished . . . She swallowed. She wished she hadn't let him inside. But she'd had no choice, had she? It would have been totally unreasonable to deny him the use of her phone. But having him here, inside her home, made her feel so exposed, so strangely vulnerable. As if she had also admitted him into—Maggie promptly told herself that her thoughts were bordering on lunacy. "I'll call Paula for you, Dr. Wilder," she repeated in what she hoped was a take-charge, no-nonsense tone of voice.

"Not Dr. Wilder. Greg," he corrected her. He'd asked her to call him Greg a year or so ago, but she never had. "Call me Greg. I call you Maggie, don't I? Is it short for Margaret?"

"I wish it were, but it's short for Mary Magdalene." Maggie imparted this information reluctantly. "When my brothers wanted to infuriate me, that's what they would call me."

Greg's lips twitched with amusement. "Then I guess I'd better stick to Maggie." He'd always known she had nice legs, he thought as his gaze swept the length of her limbs. Long, shapely, slim. He'd noticed them before, but now he wanted to touch them, to run his hand along their silken length. A flash of heat swept through him and he tried to shake off the thought.

Kevin and Joshua burst into the kitchen, fortunately diverting him. "We want a snack!" Josh boomed, then caught sight of his father and stopped in his tracks. "What are you doing here, Dad?"

Greg raised his brows and asked a question of his own. "You were asking Mrs. May for something to eat, Joshua?"

Josh looked at his shoes. "Uh, yeah."

"You aren't to ask for food at someone else's house, Joshua. You're to wait until it's offered to you. You know that," Greg reproved his son. "And you weren't even asking politely. You were demanding!"

"He was just kidding, Dr. Wilder," Kevin interjected quickly. "Sometimes we joke around like that with my mother. She doesn't mind, do you, Mom?"

"No." Maggie smiled at the boys. "I promised Kev and Josh that they could make some popcorn and I think that's what they came down to do." Both boys nodded in agreement. The car horn blared again.

"Who keeps honking that horn?" Kevin asked, frowning. "Mr. Crothers is going to get mad and call the police if it keeps up."

Greg cleared his throat. "Maybe you'd better make that call to Paula for me, Maggie, if you're sure you don't mind." Damn Francine! He wished he could make her disappear and the car horn along with her.

Greg was shaken by the sheer force of his anger. He was feeling no pleasure at the thought of an evening with Francine. The prospect of watching Maggie and the kids pop corn in her too-small kitchen held infinitely greater appeal. His eyes fastened on a strand of hair that had escaped from her ponytail and curled against the nape of her neck. It took every ounce of willpower he possessed to keep from reaching out and touching the bright auburn wisps. Her neck was graceful and slender and he wondered if the skin was as soft as it looked. But he didn't dare touch her. If he did, Maggie would be shocked out of that creamy, silken skin. She didn't see him as a man; he was just a daddy to her, the Wilder kids' daddy. She didn't even call him Greg. Dr. Wilder. Always Dr. Wilder. Suddenly that fact irritated him enormously. He wondered if he would ever gain admittance to her home again, or if he'd be relegated back to the infernal doorstep. *That* idea was absolutely intolerable to him.

Maggie saw him scowl and wondered what fate awaited the impetuous Francine. Of course, a woman as beautiful and sexy as Francine would probably have ways of creatively channeling a man's anger into something else entirely. Casting another covert glance at Greg, Maggie found herself wondering what it would be like to coax him out of his anger into . . . something else entirely. He had a sensual mouth, wide and generous, the lower lip curved and full. And his hands were surgeon's hands, big and strong and capable, with long fingers and squared, immaculate nails. What would it be like to be touched by those hands, to feel that mouth on hers? What if *she* were the one leaving for a night out with Greg, and Francine were staying behind to mind the children?

The direction her thoughts had taken unnerved Maggie and she felt a slow blush spread over her skin. She didn't indulge in erotic fantasies very often. In fact, she'd thought the sexual side of her was well and truly dead. Since Johnny's death she had stopped thinking of herself as a sexual woman. She was a mommy, a sexless, thoroughly maternal mother of three. And there was no man in her life to prove otherwise. She'd learned long ago that a woman accompanied by children was invisible to the public at large and to men in particular. People might glance at the children, but they never saw the mother. Not even men in hard hats at construction sites whistled or leered at a woman with children by her side. And Maggie seldom went anywhere or did anything without her kids.

She was thankful that Greg Wilder was unaware of her wayward thoughts. Wouldn't he be stunned to know that the Perfect Mother—and therefore the Asexual Being—was having a lascivious thought or two about him? He would be heartily sorry he'd ever set foot in her kitchen!

Maggie grinned in spite of herself. She watched Greg ruffle Joshua's hair, then do the same to Kevin. Josh stiffened; Kevin beamed. He was always thrilled by masculine attention, however slight. Enterprising Kevin had managed to assemble a whole cast of surrogate fathers for himself.

"Tell Max and Wendy I want to say goodnight to them," Greg said to Josh.

Josh gave a reluctant shrug. "I'll tell them, Dr. Wilder," Kevin said, and rushed from the kitchen. He appeared with Max and Wendy in tow a few moments later.

Maggie watched Greg kiss Wendy's cheek and give Max a quick hug. It was a heartwarming sight, seeing a father's affection for his children.

Max squirmed away with a glare at his father and ran from the kitchen. "I guess he's still angry with me," Greg said with a small smile. But his eyes were sad.

Suddenly it was difficult for Maggie to swallow around the lump that had risen in her throat. She led Greg to the door, wondering what on earth was the matter with her.

"Good night, Maggie," Greg said softly. The burgundy Cadillac loomed before them with Francine ensconced inside. Maggie mumbled a response and quickly closed the door.

Two

Maggie was in the kitchen at eight-fifteen the next morning making pancakes for the children, who were gathered around the television set watching cartoons.

"Good morning!" boomed a deep masculine voice.

Maggie was so startled, she jumped and dropped the spatula and the pancake she was flipping. "Dr. Wilder!" She whirled around to find Greg standing a few feet away, dressed casually in wheat-colored jeans and a navy and yellow striped rugby shirt.

"I'm sorry I startled you, Maggie. Kristin told me to come right in." He was feeling inordinately pleased with himself. Young Kristin hadn't tried to detain him even momentarily on the doorstep. He was inside again and he felt charged with an aggressive, triumphant energy.

Maggie stooped to retrieve the spatula, then tossed the unfortunate pancake into the sink. "I didn't expect you so early this morning, Dr. Wilder." A mild understatement. She'd thought he would sleep till noon with the lovely Francine. She'd thought about it quite a bit, much to her annoyance. "I'm sorry, but the children aren't dressed yet and they haven't had their breakfast and I—" She glanced down at the thin, yellow cotton robe which covered the matching sleeveless nightie. Both ended several inches above her knees. Her dark auburn hair hung loose around her face and she quickly flicked two strands behind her ears. "I—We just got up about fifteen minutes ago." She felt oddly breathless and very embarrassed to be caught looking this way. And she was totally disconcerted by Greg's presence in her home. He seemed to take over the small kitchen and dwarf it; the atmosphere seemed to crackle with tension. She wished she could think of something hilarious to say to break that peculiar tension, but wit failed her.

"I'm still getting used to working during the day and sleeping at night, I think," she blurted out. Hardly a bon mot.

"You don't work the night shift anymore? You worked for the airlines, I believe. In Washington?"

"Baltimore," she corrected him. "And I don't work there. I quit in August, right before school began this term. There was an opening for a secretary at the Woodland Elementary School office and the principal offered me the job. A payoff for the hundreds of cookies I've baked over the years, perhaps." She smiled and Greg laughed appreciatively at her little joke.

Encouraged, she went on. "Since Kari was to begin first grade this fall, I wanted a daytime job, and this one was perfect for me. I have the same hours as the kids, the same days off, and after working nights all those years . . ." Shut up, Maggie, she admonished herself. You're babbling, and boring the poor man to death.

"Does your new job pay better than your job with the airlines?" Greg asked politely. He was too gentlemanly to act as bored as he undoubtedly felt, Maggie decided. "I imagine it was difficult to give up those great travel benefits, regardless of pay," he added.

"The kids and I never went anywhere, anyway." The airlines might provide almost free passage, but they didn't pick up the tab for vacation expenses, and

Maggie couldn't afford to either. "The school pays less, but the hours make it worth it. I just take on more baby-sitting. We're managing all right," she felt compelled to inform him.

"Well, I do envy you sleeping till eight." Greg smiled at her. "I've been up since a quarter to six. I've already made rounds at the hospital, and since the boys have a soccer game at ten, I thought I'd bring over Josh's uniform and clothes for Max and Wendy too."

Maggie suddenly noticed the canvas bag he was carrying. "I—I wasn't expecting you," she repeated inanely. He looked so vital, so strikingly, aggressively male. She drew back against the counter, horribly aware of her uncombed hair, her lack of makeup, and the faded, too-thin nightclothes. She knew she looked a wreck, probably worse than she'd looked the night before. His odd stare seemed to confirm her supposition. She swallowed hard. He was very near. Never had the kitchen seemed so small. "I'd planned to take the boys to the soccer game," she said, aware she was starting to babble again. "Josh was going to wear Kevin's spare uniform and I'd planned to outfit Wendy and Max in—Oh!"

The smell of burning pancakes drew her attention to the skillet, where the charred remains were beginning to smolder. "What a mess!" she groaned, dumping the contents into the sink. "I'm simply not my best in the morning, I'm afraid."

"Especially when you've been scared out of your wits by an unexpected visitor," Greg added dryly.

She began to scrub the skillet. He must think her an air-headed fool! "It'll just take me a few minutes to whip up another batch of batter and then I'll feed the kids." She hoped she sounded a little more competent. What was the matter with her this morning anyway? She'd been making pancakes for years and had never burnt them before. She knew the answer, of course. Greg Wilder was the cause of her nervous bumbling. She was too aware of him to pay attention to anything else.

"Would I be overstepping my bounds if I asked if you had enough pancake batter to feed one more?" he asked ingenuously. "I know I lectured Josh about waiting until food was offered, but . . ." He gave her a disarming smile, and Maggie was totally disarmed.

"Would you like some pancakes, Dr. Wilder?" she asked in a breathless rush. "There's plenty of batter."

"Greg," he corrected, and settled himself in one of the vinyl-covered kitchen chairs. "And I accept your generous offer. I can't even remember the last time I had a home-cooked breakfast. I either eat some of the kids' junk cereal at home on the run or grab some of the hospital cafeteria's lethal donuts and coffee."

"I'm not much of a breakfast eater myself." Maggie mixed the eggs and flour and milk together, very aware that he was watching her work. She desperately wished she were dressed. Knowing that she was naked beneath her gown . . . She whipped the batter feverishly with a fork in an effort to distract herself from her thoughts. As if Greg Wilder noticed or even cared what she was—or wasn't—wearing. Particularly after his passionate night with the sexy Francine. He would hardly speculate about his children's baby-sitter, a widowed mother of three. The man was a doctor, a father!

"Josh will be delighted that you're coming to the game this morning, Dr. Wilder," she said with extreme brightness. "He—"

"Greg," he interrupted. "Remember?"

Maggie's cheeks grew warm. She remembered. She'd thought of him as Greg for a long time, but determinedly forced herself to maintain the distancing "Dr. Wilder." She didn't know why. Her hands were trembling as she poured the batter into the skillet. "Josh and Kevin were kicking the soccer ball around in the yard yesterday. They're determined to win their game today." She deliberately turned to the topic of the children in an attempt to dissipate her ridiculous anxiety. She felt safe and comfortable in her mommy role. "Max was playing with them for a while too. You should see him kick the ball! He seems to have a natural flair for it. I guess you'll be signing him up for soccer next year when he turns five?"

"I'm sure I will."

She glanced at him, wondering at the odd note in his voice. Her eyes collided with his and she drew her breath in sharply. He had the most gorgeous eyes, she thought for perhaps the thousandth time. That rich, unusual color, those dark, thick lashes . . .

"Your eyes are really green," Greg said, and Maggie blinked in confusion. She had been thinking of *his* eyes. To hear him comment on her own totally flummoxed her.

"I don't think I've ever seen truly green eyes," he went on. "Usually what passes for green is a combination of green and hazel or blue or brown. But your eyes are definitely green, almost an emerald shade. Lovely," he added, almost as an afterthought.

"Thank you." She turned her attention to the pancakes, aware that her heart was pounding. And she'd been worried about Kristin and Kari's reactions to a man! Her own were pitiable; she'd had more poise as a teenager in high school. Put a man in her kitchen today and she nearly fell apart. Add a compliment from him and she was reduced to a quivering mass of nerves. Maggie was thoroughly disgusted with herself.

"Green eyes and auburn hair," Greg said musingly. He was still studying her. Maggie was rigidly aware of his gaze upon her. "What was your maiden name, Maggie?"

"O'Reilly," she replied in a tight little voice. "It's Irish," she added unnecessarily.

"I see." Greg was smiling a smile that made her feel weak. "Mary Magdalene O'Reilly. When did your family begin to call you Maggie?"

"About fifteen seconds after birth, thank heavens." She piled a stack of pancakes onto a plate and set it in front of Greg, along with the butter and five bottles of syrup.

"Strawberry, blueberry, raspberry, boysenberry, and maple," he said, reading each label. "What a choice! I'm impressed, Maggie. This is just like the House of Pancakes."

"Everyone in our family likes a different flavor." She was standing beside him at the table, close enough to smell his fresh, woodsy after-shave. She quickly backed away.

"Delicious," he said appreciatively, sampling a bite. He had unstacked his pancakes and poured a different syrup on each one.

"You eat your pancakes just like Max," she said, smiling at the similarity. "He likes to try all the flavors too."

"I wasn't aware that Max had ever eaten breakfast here before." Greg looked puzzled by his apparent memory lapse.

"Oh, he hasn't. But sometimes I make him pancakes for dinner when he hates what the rest of us are having. And occasionally he requests them for an after-school snack."

"And you indulge him? You're exceptionally kind, Maggie." Greg paused to stare up at her. "I . . . want to thank you for being so good to Max. And to Josh and Wendy too. You've been a stabilizing, positive influence in their lives and I appreciate it very much."

She flushed, uneasy with his praise and his thanks. "I'll take the plates into the kids." She was grateful for the diversion. "They like to eat in front of the TV so they don't miss a minute of the Smurfs." She left the kitchen carrying two plates of pancakes. To her surprise, Greg followed her with the third.

"Company first," Maggie said, giving Wendy and Max each a plate and a fork. She set up the syrup bottles on the coffee table.

"Ladies first," corrected Greg, bypassing Josh to

give the plate he held to Kari. Maggie was ridiculously pleased by the small gesture.

Kari beamed up at him. "I have a loose tooth," she said shyly, wiggling her lower front tooth for him. It was the first time, to Maggie's knowledge, that Kari had initiated a conversation with a man. In the light of her worries about her daughters, it was a welcome occurrence.

Greg felt the tooth. "It's loose all right," he said. "But not quite ready to come out." He flicked one of the little girl's long blond braids over her shoulder. "You have the longest pigtails I've ever seen. Haven't you ever had your hair cut?"

Kari shook her head. "Wendy wishes her hair was long." She stared up at him. "How come you make her get it cut so short?"

Maggie glanced at Wendy, who was sitting quietly eating her pancakes. The little girl's boyishly short bowl cut was not particularly flattering to her small, thin face. Maggie had long thought that Greg probably took Josh, Wendy, and Max to one barber who gave all three identical cuts.

"Wendy, you never told me you wanted your hair long," Greg said. He seemed bewildered by Kari's pronouncement. "You don't have to have it cut if you don't want to."

Wendy said nothing. "Mom, Josh and I are starving," complained Kevin. "Where's our pancakes?"

"I'll make yours next, right away," Maggie promised, smiling as Josh rolled around on the floor in a dramatic bout of mock hunger pangs. "I'll make yours a double batch."

"Better hurry, Mom. I don't know how long these poor starving fellows will last without food," kidded Greg. He fastened his hand around the nape of Maggie's neck and pointed her toward the kitchen. "Forward, march!"

Maggie's heart seemed to lurch, then ricochet wildly against her rib cage. The feel of the warm hand on her neck, the touch of his fingers against her skin, had an alarming effect on her senses. The blood drummed madly in her head and she took a deep, steadying breath. What on earth was the matter with her? she thought. Greg was joking with her; he meant nothing by his casual touch.

But her physical response to that casual touch grew stronger. The taut fluttering in her abdomen was unmistakably sexual arousal, something that she hadn't experienced for ages. And a quick glance down at the front of her nightgown confirmed what she already knew. Her nipples were tingling and tightening and clearly visible under the thin cotton.

"Mom!" Kristin ran down the stairs, petite and cute in a pale blue leotard and jeans. Her hair, an auburn several shades lighter than Maggie's, was pulled into two short ponytails and tied with blue ribbons. She came to a screeching halt in front of her mother and Maggie had to stop suddenly, causing Greg, who was walking closely behind her, to collide with her.

The impact of his hard frame sent shock waves of sensation through her already sensitized body. His hand slid from her neck and both arms came around to encircle her in an attempt to restore their balance. Maggie felt the strength of his chest against her back, the muscular thighs against her bottom, his strong arms around her waist. He might be trying to balance her, but she had never felt more *off balance* in her entire life.

"I'm off, Mommy. Wish me luck," Kristin said blithely, seemingly oblivious to the sight of her mother in a man's arms.

But then, she wasn't really in Greg's arms, Maggie tried to assure herself. She had stopped suddenly and he had crashed into her. And being a gentleman—and a doctor and a father, she added in an attempt to calm herself—he had helped her to regain her equilibrium. *That* was the sight Kristin saw. The Wilder kids' dad lending support to her mom.

"Where are you off to, Kristin?" Greg asked pleasantly. He had not yet released Maggie. He remained close behind her, their bodies touching, his arms firmly around her. He locked his hands together over the slight swell of her stomach. Her head didn't quite reach his shoulder and his breath ruffled her hair as he spoke.

"I have a gymnastic meet at ten," Kristin replied shyly. "But I'm leaving early to practice at the Community Center."

"Gymnastic meet, hmm? Who are you competing against?" he asked. Maggie wriggled slightly in an effort to break free, but he didn't release her. His big hands were warm against her abdomen, causing a throbbing within. There didn't seem to be a part of her not touching him. Her nipples were aching and became more pronounced, and there was a taut heat between her thighs.

"We're competing against the Columbia Community Center's team," Kristin was telling Greg. She seemed pleased by his interest. "A bus will take us over there and bring us back. Columbia is very good. They really beat us last year, but we've been practicing all summer and we've won our last two meets. I hope we beat them this time."

"I hope so too, Kristin," Greg said heartily. "And I wish you the best of luck."

Kristin blushed. "Thanks, Dr. Wilder."

"Kristin!" chorused three similarly attired young gymnasts who had arrived at the screen door. "Are you ready to go?"

Greg unlocked his hands and Maggie rushed to the door where Kristin had already admitted her friends. Maggie couldn't remember ever being so glad to see them. "Hi Jen, Hi Jenny, Hi Jennifer," she greeted them.

"Hi, Mrs. May," the girls answered in unison.

"Do you have time for a quick snack?" Maggie asked hopefully.

"Not now, Mom," replied Kristin.

"We'll take you up on it later, Mrs. May," one of the Jennifers added.

Kristin gave her mother a quick kiss on the cheek and the little group departed, calling their good-byes. And leaving Maggie alone with Greg. "I hope they win today, they try so hard," she said, staring out the screen door.

"I hope they win too," Greg said. "I never realized how much Kristin looks like you, Maggie. The same wide-set green eyes, the same nose turned up with a smattering of freckles. And almost the same hair color. You—" He broke off and Maggie glanced over at him, only to find his gaze riveted to her body.

A quick glance down at herself revealed why. She was standing in the sunlight and every curve of her body was visible through her now translucent robe and nightgown. Her nipples pointed boldly outward and Greg stared at them. Maggie's mouth was dry and she wanted to sink with mortification. Darting from the revealing shaft of sunlight, she sought refuge in the shadow of the staircase.

Greg followed her to stand at the foot of the stairs as Maggie backed up a step. His gaze had shifted and she drew a shaky breath of relief. It was time to remind them both of their proper roles of mother and father. Their *safe* roles. "Can you believe that Kristin's three best friends are all named Jennifer?" she said. "We call two of them Jen and Jenny just to keep them straight."

Greg smiled and said nothing and Maggie felt compelled to rattle on. "Jennifer was the number one girl's name in America the year that Kristin was born. We, Johnny and I, briefly considered it ourselves, but when four couples we knew *and* my brother and his wife had baby girls that year and named them Jennifer, we switched to Kristin. Kristin Jennifer." She was talking too much and too fast. When she lifted her eyes from the third button on his rugby shirt and stole a look at his face, she found Greg smiling in a reminiscent way.

"Jennifer was the number one name the year Paula was born too. And I must confess, Alicia and I also considered it. But, like you, we knew too many couples with Jennifers born that year so we went with Paula Jennifer."

They both laughed at that. She liked the way Greg's eyes sparkled when he laughed, Maggie realized, staring into the warm aquamarine depths. And the way he smiled was incredibly appealing. Swallowing, she took another step backward. "If you'll excuse me a moment, Greg—uh, Dr. Wilder—I'll just run upstairs and get dressed." She was already slowly backing up the stairs as she spoke. She *had* to escape from the overwhelming potency of his attraction, to regain her already shattered composure.

"The boys aren't going to want to wait for their pancakes," Greg warned.

"Oh, this will only take a minute." She backed up another step, putting her halfway to the top, and carefully folded her arms in front of her chest to cover herself.

He put one foot on the bottom stair. "I make you nervous, don't I, Maggie?"

She was floored by his bluntness. "N-no! Of course not!" Her voice was too shrill, too high.

He went up another step. "Then why are you running away? You've been backing up those stairs the way one would back away from a cobra."

Her face was scarlet. "I—I told you that I want to get dressed. I don't like schlepping around in my robe all day, that's all."

"I'd hardly say you were guilty of that. It's not quite nine o'clock. A lot of people aren't even out of bed at this hour on a Saturday morning."

"I'm surprised that *you* are," she blurted out, and was promptly horrified with herself. She couldn't really have said that!

Greg picked up instantly on her allusion. "You thought I'd take advantage of my children's absence and spend the morning in bed with Francine Gallier?"

Maggie was flustered by his accurate guess. "You have every right to do what you want, Dr. Wilder," she said hastily. She didn't want him to think her a condemning prude! "You are both consenting adults and—"

"Not after last night," he interrupted grimly. "I wouldn't consent to a damn thing with that cold-blooded bitch."

Maggie stared at him, nonplussed. "You . . . didn't have a good time last night?" Her curiosity momentarily overrode her embarrassment, modesty, and inhibitions. She unconsciously took one step down, forgetting to keep her arms crossed in front of her.

"A good time? Ha! The evening went downhill from the moment we left here."

If the evening had deteriorated from blaring horns and Greg's tight-lipped fury, Maggie thought, they must have hit new depths of rancor. The pits, as Kristin would say, and Maggie wasn't altogether displeased by the notion.

"What happened?" she dared to ask, wondering if she was being presumptuous or nosy and deciding that she was definitely being both.

"First of all, I didn't appreciate her leaning on the car horn while I made arrangements for my children's care," Greg said with a self-righteous sniff that made Maggie smile. "Then, as we were both fuming along Route 8, I started to think about Max jumping her the way he did. Now, I realize that Max may be a pain at times"—Greg took another step up and Maggie took one down, both seemingly unaware of their actions—"but he has never attacked anyone without some sort of provocation. So I asked Francine what she'd said to Max to make him react so violently."

"Did she tell you?"

"She became so defensive that I *knew* she'd said something terrible to him. When I finally got it out of her, I was so furious, I could scarcely speak." He clenched his fists, his eyes darkening at the memory. "I took her back to her place and told her to get out of the car, that I was going home. I think she got my message."

"I should think so," Maggie said dryly.

"Do you know what she said to Max?"

She nodded tentatively. She well understood his parental rage.

"She threatened to throw his teddy bear into the Potomac!" Greg's voice was indignant with anger. "What kind of a woman talks that way to a small child? It was a cruel and sadistic threat, particularly knowing how attached he is to that bear, and I told her so. I have no intention of ever seeing that woman again."

Was he sorry about that? Maggie wondered. Perhaps he wasn't now, in the heat of his anger, but later on, would he come to miss the sexy Francine? "You might change your mind and make up with her again," she heard herself say and wondered why on earth she had said it. She knew why the moment she heard his reply.

"Make up with her? Why would I want to do that? I haven't been dating her long and certainly not exclusively. And I have no intention of wasting a minute of my time on a woman heartless enough to terrorize a child. My child!" he added vehemently.

She'd wanted to hear him say that, Maggie realized with dawning awareness. Hearing Greg reject the beautiful Francine was music to her ears. She gave him a beatific smile.

"After I rid myself of Francine, I drove home and took Paula to her girlfriend's house to spend the night," he continued. "Then I went back home, switched on the answering machine, and went to bed."

"I got your machine when I tried to call Paula for

you last night," Maggie said. "I left a message on it for her."

"I know. I heard it this morning."

Somehow they were only standing one step apart, Maggie above and Greg below. But because of his height, she still had to look up to him. Their eyes met and held for a long moment. A sharp pang of sensual awareness sent hot sparks shooting through her body. For that moment, neither spoke or moved. It was as if the two of them were waiting, waiting for something to happen.

Greg was first to break the strange silence. "I believe we were talking about why I make you so nervous. Before we were sidetracked, that is." He gave her a thoughtful look. "Did you do it deliberately, Maggie? Turn the subject to Francine to divert my attention from you?"

"Of course not!" She hadn't, had she?

"Then you don't mind my attentions?"

Her eyes widened at the unexpected huskiness of his voice. Before she could move or utter a sound, she was in his arms. "Dr. Wilder!" she managed to gasp.

He laughed softly. "Greg. I'm not your doctor."

"Greg, you—"

"That's right. Greg. It isn't so hard to say, is it?"

"Let me g—"

He silenced her by lightly covering her lips with his fingers, all the while holding her firmly against his long, hard frame. Maggie's first shocked instinct was to break away, but his grip was far too secure to permit it. Next came the reflexive urge to fight, to hit out at him, but her hands were caught between her chest and his, rendering them useless.

"Relax," he murmured, removing his fingers as he lowered his head. His lips hovered an inch above her own. "I'm not going to hurt you, Maggie."

"The children," she protested weakly. Her breathing was so shallow and erratic that she was perilously close to hyperventilating.

"Yes, the children. You're perfectly safe with a

houseful of kids," he said huskily, feathering kisses along the sensitive curve of her neck. His lips teased at the corner of her mouth and his big hands moved up to cup the rounded fullness of her breasts. A nervous little whimper escaped her throat.

"Don't be afraid of me, Maggie." His voice was gentle. It was the way he said her name that melted all traces of resistance within her. So softly, so sexily. She gazed up at him and was lost in the warmth of his gaze.

"I want to kiss you, Maggie. I've wanted to from the moment I saw you this morning, all tousled and sleepy-eyed."

"I'm a wreck in the morning," she said, her voice unconsciously throaty. She felt strangely suspended from reality, as if her real self were watching a scene involving some other woman, her look-alike alter ego, in the arms of Greg Wilder.

"You look incredibly sexy in the morning," he disagreed. "I wanted to carry you right back to bed. And crawl in with you." Maggie shivered at his evocative words. His hands smoothed the curve of her hips, molding her to his taut thighs. "You don't have a damn thing on under this," he growled, cupping her buttocks and kneading them with long, sensuous fingers. He buried his face in the curve of her neck.

"You smell so good, Maggie." His voice was low and intimate. "Like soap and talc and woman." Maggie felt herself go weak and soft as a seductive lethargy spread slowly through her body.

He raised his head to look down at her and her gaze flew to his face. She was captivated by his strong masculine features, the straight nose, the sensual mouth, the firm set of his jaw. He exuded a compelling virility of which she was excitingly aware. His eyes met hers and she found herself unable to look away. Those eyes, large and clear and the color of aquamarines, held her captive as steadfastly as his hands on her body. Those eyes regarded her with an unmistakable passion, traveling over the curvaceous lines of her figure, devouring the full breasts and the womanly curves of her hips and thighs.

Now holding her eyes with his, he slipped his hand between the buttons of her robe and under her nightgown. The touch of his fingers on the soft flesh of her breast jolted her as stunningly as a bolt of electricity. He caught her aching nipple between his thumb and forefinger and massaged it with a slow, sensual rhythm.

"When I saw your nipples so tight, so aroused, I wanted to touch them like this," he said raspingly. "And like this . . ." He replaced his fingers with his mouth, dampening the cloth with his tongue.

Maggie moaned as a wild excitement churned within her. She felt the sharp nip of his teeth and gasped at the erotic mixture of pleasure and pain. Tangling her fingers in the thickness of his hair, she pulled his head closer.

"You're very sensitive there, sweet Maggie." Greg lifted his head to stare down at her half-closed lids and parted lips. "I want to know all your most sensitive places." His hand ran smoothly down her belly and rested on the material covering the downy softness of tangled curls. "I want to touch you everywhere, to feel you throb and ache for me."

She arched herself closer, a small, sensuous sound escaping from her. She wanted him to touch her there, without the restricting barrier of cotton. "You are so wonderfully responsive," he whispered against her ear, his tongue tracing its soft pink shape.

He thrust his knee between her thighs and a heated urgency swept through her. Maggie's mind reeled, her body coming alive with sensations and emotions she had thought long dead. A wildfire seemed to blaze through her veins, awakening needs that had lain dormant and suppressed for so very long. Greg's mouth closed over hers and she sighed, opening her own mouth to deepen the kiss, welcoming his tongue with her own. Her body was governed by a will of its own; as if of their own volition, her arms went around his neck to hold him closer. Her breasts strained against the broad warmth of his chest and she provocatively rubbed against him. The deep, drugging kiss went on and on, rendering her pliant and mindless. When Greg lifted her off her feet and carried her to the top of the stairs, she sighed and clung to him.

"Mommy!"

The sound of a child's voice brought them both back to earth with a heartstopping thud. Maggie's eyes flew open to meet Greg's.

"Mommy!" It was Kevin and he sounded angry. His voice grew nearer and Maggie became frantically aware of her position—in Greg's arms and a perilous few feet from her bedroom.

"Put me down," she said in a choked voice, and Greg obliged, setting her gently on her feet. He reached for her, but she jerked wildly away from him and started down the stairs. She was so shaken and off-balance that she stumbled and would have fallen the rest of the way down if Greg hadn't grabbed her.

"Careful, honey." His mouth was at her ear, his warm breath fanning her neck.

"Don't!" Her voice was little more than a hoarse squeak. She tried to shrug off his hands, but they remained firmly affixed to her shoulders.

Kevin appeared at the foot of the stairs, his arms folded across his chest, his dark blue eyes blazing. "Where's my breakfast?" he demanded, all traces of his usual amiability gone. "You said you were going to fix it right away."

"I don't think that's any way to talk to your mother, Kevin," Greg said. His voice was pleasant enough, but the edge of steel in it was unmistakable.

Maggie was still dizzy from the stunning shock of her and Greg's passionate encounter. She had to fight against an almost overwhelming urge to close her eyes and lean back into his inviting strength. She took a deep breath and tried to concentrate on the little scene before her.

Kevin had been momentarily taken aback by Greg's mild reprimand. His arms dropped and his eyes widened. "I—I'm hungry," he said defensively.

"Then why not try, 'May I have my breakfast, please?'" suggested Greg. Kevin swallowed and said nothing.

"Kevin turns into the Incredible Hulk when he's hungry," Maggie said. She made it to the foot of the stairs and put her arm around her son's shoulders. "He's very good-natured almost all of the time, but if he's hungry and doesn't get his food on time, he starts snarling and stomping. He falls apart. He's been that way since he was a tiny baby." She was aware that she was being dreadfully talkative but she couldn't seem to stop. Nor could she look at Greg. What must he think of her? she thought with horror. What had happened to her? He had touched her and she had simply gone up in flames, losing all sense of time and place and *morals!* She'd been about to let him carry her to bed and make love to her with five small children downstairs!

"Mom, may I have my breakfast, please?" Kevin asked politely, glancing up at Greg. He gave the boy an approving smile which Kevin returned.

"Of course, darling." Maggie stumbled blindly toward the kitchen, still holding onto her son. The child was a comforting anchor of reality to her—and his presence kept her torturous thoughts at bay. "I'll fix you and Josh some pancakes right now."

"Me and Wendy," Kevin corrected her. "Josh isn't hungry anymore. He ate all Wendy's pancakes. But Kari wouldn't give me hers," he added with an injured air. "Sometimes I wish I could trade sisters."

Greg chuckled, making Maggie aware that he had followed them into the kitchen. She wished he hadn't. She wished he would disappear. What was she going to say to him? Worse, her body was still throbbing with the excitement of his caresses. His voice sent a pleasurable tingle down her spine.

"We'll bring your pancakes into you in a few minutes, Kevin," he said. "Why don't you watch your program while you're waiting? We won't be long."

"Okay," Kevin said, pacified for the moment. He raced off and Maggie almost called after him and begged him to stay. She did *not* want to be alone with Greg Wilder.

"Maggie." She ignored the sexy, intimate drawl and began tossing ingredients into the bowl, haphazardly guessing at the correct amounts. "Maggie, turn around and look at me."

She couldn't. She simply couldn't.

"Mary Magdalene!" His voice, though amused, held a commanding note.

"Don't call me that!" she said in a sudden flash of anger.

He was beside her now and she was shatteringly aware of his nearness, of the strength and virility emanating from him. "You wouldn't answer to Maggie. I had to get your attention somehow."

She could feel his eyes upon her as she reached for another egg. Still, she couldn't bring herself to turn around and look at him. And then his hand was on her neck, the long fingers gently stroking. "Maggie?" he murmured softly.

She dropped the egg and it splattered all over the counter. "That was my last egg!" she wailed. She tried to salvage what she could of it, scraping it up while avoiding the little pieces of shell. Actually, she was grateful for the diversion. "I need it for this batter. If Kevin has to wait any longer for his breakfast, he'll—"

Greg caught her chin with his other hand and forced her to look up at him. "Forget Kevin's breakfast for a minute, Maggie. And forget the stupid egg. Why won't you look at me? Why won't you talk to me?"

"Let me go!" She tried to wrench away from him, humiliatingly aware that her behavior bordered on the adolescent. He had kissed her and she should have reacted with blasé cool. She knew that, but she couldn't seem to help her histrionic response. "Go in and watch television with the kids," she snapped in an effort to regain her lost composure. "I have to make Kevin's breakfast. He's hungry and—"

"It's a mother's duty to feed her little ones," Greg finished nobly. He cast her a playfully rakish grin, which, to her dismay, she found utterly irresistible. "But it's a woman's job to satisfy her man," he added, teasing. Before she could move, speak, or even breathe, he hauled her into his arms. "Now where were we?" He grabbed a handful of her hair and gently tilted her head upward.

Three

"Stop it, Greg!" Maggie's heart was racing and she fought the treacherous urge to relax against him. She couldn't succumb to him twice! She pushed at his chest with renewed determination. "If you don't let me go immediately, I'll—I'll call all the kids into the kitchen."

Greg laughed. "Now there's a threat! All five of them stampeding in, demanding food or drink or popsicles at the top of their powerful little lungs." He released her and held up his hands. "See? You're free. So don't sic the, er, little darlings on me."

Maggie moved briskly away from him and began to beat the batter viciously with a fork.

"Maggie, what is it?" Greg asked quietly, all traces of humor gone from his voice. "Tell me." He touched a lock of her auburn hair. It was as soft and silky as it looked. And so was her skin. He wondered how he had managed to keep from touching her all this time. And now that he had touched her, it was difficult to restrain himself from reaching out again and pulling her back into his arms. But he knew he must. Their passionate interlude on the stairs had clearly shocked her. It had shocked him as well. He'd never dreamed their responses to each other would be so incredibly volatile, so wildly exciting.

"I didn't mean to rush you," he said, fighting off

the desire to rush her again. When they had been standing so closely on the stairs he'd recognized her attraction to him. It was almost as if permitting him into her house had allowed her to let down her emotional barriers as well. She was suddenly sexually aware of him and he'd been unable to resist responding to her.

"I'm not what you—you probably think I am," she said stiffly, jerking her head away from his touch. Her hair fell against her cheek. "I—I'm not a sex-starved widow looking for a cheap thrill."

There was an ominous silence and Maggie gathered enough courage to cast a covert glance at Greg. He was grinning! "What's so funny?" she demanded, pouring oil into the hot skillet. It spit back at her and she lowered the temperature slightly before spooning the batter into the pan.

"You are. A sex-starved widow looking for a cheap thrill."

"I'm not!" she said hotly. "How dare you say such a thing!"

He laughed at her indignation. "I've never seen you this way. You're cute when you're all fired up, Maggie." He lounged comfortably against the counter, obviously enormously amused.

"A not-very-clever spin-off of the tired, old 'You're beautiful when you're angry' line," she muttered. She'd watched enough TV to know all about tired, old lines. "Surely a man of your vast experience can do better than that, *Dr. Wilder.*"

"So we're back to that, hmm? Funny how you didn't seem to have any trouble saying Greg back there on the steps, *Mrs. May.*"

"Don't call me that!" Maggie snapped, then paused to stare at him, confused. There was absolutely nothing wrong with Greg addressing her as Mrs. May. Except that she hated him to do it. "I mean I—you—"

"You don't know what you mean, hot little Maggie," Greg replied, laughing. He was positively delighted that he'd managed to shake her previously relentless cordiality toward him.

Her cheeks burned. "Don't laugh at me!"

"I'm not laughing at you." He traced the length of her arm with one long finger, slightly scoring her skin with his nail. To her great dismay, Maggie quivered at even this most simple touch. Greg was watching her, his eyes narrowed speculatively.

She stepped away from him. "Greg, I know I'm acting like a blazing idiot." She chewed her lower lip. This was incredibly difficult for her. "But I'm not well versed in these—these games. You're the first man who's kissed me since my husband died."

Greg looked stunned. "You're kidding!" he said.

For some reason, his reaction infuriated her. "No, I'm not," she replied defiantly. "You're the first. And I'm sorry that it had to be you."

His lips tightened into a straight, hard line. "Why?" he asked harshly.

"Why?" she echoed crossly. "I'll tell you why, *Dr. Wilder.* You had a fight with your girlfriend last night and you went to bed all frustrated and—and—" She swallowed. "Unsatisfied. When you woke up this morning in the same unfortunate condition, you grabbed the first woman you saw. And it happened to be me! Am I supposed to be flattered by your attentions? Well, I'm not!"

"Maggie, you're wrong. I—"

"I'm absolutely right and I refuse to discuss it any further."

"Oh, we're going to discuss it, Maggie. Just as soon as you finish making the children's breakfast."

Maggie flipped the pancakes onto two plates and sailed out of the kitchen, her head held high. After serving Wendy and Kevin, she hurried upstairs, ignoring Greg's commanding summons from the kitchen. She rushed into her bedroom and locked the door behind her. She'd made a complete and utter fool of herself with Greg, she conceded grimly, quickly stripping off her robe and nightgown and reaching into the drawer for her underwear. She caught a glimpse of herself in the mirror above the bureau and stared at her nude body as if seeing it for the first time. Full mature breasts—breasts that had nursed three babies—that were softly rounded with rosy peaks. Waist, not as small as it had once been, but still in proportion to her breasts and womanly curved hips. Legs long and well shaped, the thighs still firm and rounded, calves and ankles slim.

For just a moment Maggie allowed herself to remember the feel of Greg's experienced hands on her body and every nerve began to tingle. She pulled on her panties and bra with an exclamation of self-disgust. Those were the thoughts of the hot, sex-starved widow, which, as she had heatedly assured Greg, she most definitely was not! She was a respecta-ble, solicitously maternal mother of three. Her eyes fell upon a framed photograph of Kristin, Kevin, and Kari taken some four years ago. They were so little then, and how they had needed her! She thought back to the day when she had been given the terrible, tragic news of Johnny's death. Kari had been one week old, Kevin three years, and Kristin six. Numb and heartbroken, she had nevertheless carried on for her children's sake. She had lived for them and given them every bit of love, energy, and affection that she possessed. And for years it had been enough.

But the children were older now, were becoming involved in school activities and friends and interests outside their home. They didn't need their mother as much. Maggie foresaw the day when they would leave home and she would be alone, and her pain at the thought frightened her. Above all, she didn't want to be the kind of martyr-mother who clung to her chil-dren, refusing to let them go because they were the sole reason for her otherwise empty existence. It was a terrible burden to place on a child and a totally unfair one. Maggie wanted her children to feel free to grow up and become independent.

She pushed her disturbing thoughts aside. The

day her children left home was a long way off. It was foolish to brood about it now. She enjoyed her life, just as it was, and damn Greg Wilder for making her feel anything but content with her lot.

She pulled on a green and white striped blouse, a pair of blue jeans, sport socks, and sneakers, her usual Saturday uniform. Then she brushed her hair until it shone and curved around her neck in a saucy pageboy. Frowning at her reflection, she deliberately pulled the hair up into a less flattering ponytail, carefully avoiding considering her motives in doing so. After applying her makeup—for Kevin's sake, Maggie assured herself (her son wouldn't want his mother to appear at his soccer game looking as washed out as a ghost)—she headed downstairs.

Greg was in the living room with the children, holding Wendy on his lap. "It's time to get dressed and leave for the soccer game," Maggie announced to the children.

"Do I have to go?" Max whined. "I want to stay here and watch cartoons."

"I'll stay with him, Mommy," Kari volunteered. Her motives, Maggie knew, were more governed by her own desire to stay home and watch the cartoons than by any altruistic wish to take care of Max. "I'm afraid you're a little young to baby-sit anybody, Kari," she said with a smile. She glanced over at Wendy sitting impassively on her father's lap. "Your daddy brought your clothes, Wendy. You and Kari go on up to her room and change."

Compliant as always, Wendy hopped off Greg's knee, gathered her small pile of clothes, and trotted out of the room after Kari. Kevin jumped to his feet, switched off the television set, and challenged Joshua to a race upstairs. The two boys tore through the small house and the walls seemed to shake with the noise. Max glanced at Maggie and his father, calmly walked to the TV, and turned on the set. He then seated himself cross-legged directly in front of it. Greg and Maggie exchanged glances, suddenly allies in the face of Max's declaration of war.

Greg stood up. "Max, no more TV." His voice was forcedly pleasant. "It's time to get dressed and go to the soccer game."

Max didn't move. "I don't wanna go. I wanna stay here."

"Well, you can't. You're going." Greg strode to the television and turned it off. Max slipped past him and turned it on. Greg turned it off. Max turned it back on. And then they repeated themselves for one more round. The television blared defiantly.

Maggie foresaw an ungodly expensive TV repair bill. "The next one who touches that television set gets a spanking!" she warned automatically in her most intimidating mother-voice.

Max froze and stared from the blaring TV set to his father, his brown eyes gleaming. "I'll get dressed now, Maggie," he said with a sudden, angelic smile. Maggie saw Greg's shoulders sag with relief at having avoided another unpleasant confrontation with his child. He reached down and switched off the television set.

"You touched it! Daddy touched it!" Max shrieked, jumping up and down. "He gets a spanking, doesn't he, Maggie? Daddy gets a spanking!"

Greg's face reddened and he scowled his irritation. "Set up by a four-year-old!" he mumbled. Maggie couldn't help laughing and Greg's frown deepened. He obviously didn't find Max's gleeful squeals as funny as Maggie did.

"Give him a spanking, Maggie!" urged Max, grabbing her hand and pulling her toward his father. "Go on, hit 'im hard."

"The little sadist," Greg grumbled.

"Revenge is sweet, even for the very young," Maggie said. "Okay, Daddy, are you ready to take your medicine?"

"Not medicine, he's not sick," Max said. "He's bad and he needs a hard spanking."

"Shall I sit down on the sofa and take you over my knees?" Maggie was thoroughly enjoying Greg's discomfort. He was clearly not used to being at a disadvantage.

"Yeah!" Max yelled.

"I think this little joke has gone on long enough." Greg's smile was definitely forced. His face looked ready to crack. "Time to get dressed now, Max."

"Get 'im, Maggie!" cried Max.

"You really don't want me to hit your daddy, do you, Max?" Maggie wondered if things weren't getting a little out of hand. She hadn't expected Max to be so insistent. "What if I make him cry?"

"Good! He made me cry. And—and I hate that dumb lady too!" the little boy added fiercely.

"Which dumb lady?" Maggie asked. "The one in the car last night?" The plot thickens, she thought. Max hadn't forgotten the lovely Francine or his father's seeming betrayal of him and his bear. But she could put things to right. "Your daddy found out what she said about Teddy and he was so mad at her that he wouldn't take her to the party. He took her right back to her house and told her how mean he thought she was. He said he didn't want to be her friend anymore."

Max listened pensively, chewing on two of his fingers. "Your daddy loves you very much, Max," Maggie continued. "Even when you're being naughty."

Greg cleared his throat. "That's right, Max." He came to stand beside the little boy, then impulsively knelt down and hugged him. Maggie, an admittedly absurd sentimentalist, felt a quick rush of tears at the sight.

"Do you want me to help you get dressed?" Greg asked Max.

The little boy shook his head. "I can do it myself," he said. He snatched up his clothes and skipped from the room, pausing to call over his shoulder, "I guess you don't have to spank him, Maggie."

Maggie laughed. Though he was sometimes a trial, she eventually always found Max appealing.

"You handled that beautifully, Maggie," Greg said. He was staring at her in the most peculiar way.

"Sometimes a little humor can defuse a potentially explosive situation. Say, maybe I should apply for a position on the bomb squad," she joked.

Greg didn't laugh. He was still watching her, his expression enigmatic. But his eyes, alert and intelligent, seemed to be assessing her in a whole new way.

He was beginning to make her nervous again. "I'd better go and braid Kari's hair," she murmured. It was an effort not to dash out of the room, but she forced herself to walk at a normal pace.

"Maggie?" Greg's voice halted her in her tracks.

She didn't turn around. "Yes?"

"Thank you. For helping both Max and me." His voice was warm and very deep. Maggie gave a quick, acknowledging nod and rushed from the room.

The soccer game was held in the Woodland Elementary School's grassy field. Kari and Max and Wendy played on the playground equipment in the nearby schoolyard with a crowd of other children, none of them paying much attention to their brothers' game on the field. Maggie and Greg stood on the sidelines watching the game with a group of other loyal parents. It was a sunny day, breezy and cooler than yesterday's unseasonable high. True Indian summer, Maggie thought, glancing at the colored leaves on the trees that shaded the playground. Pleased to see that the younger kids were playing well together, she returned her attention to the game.

"Hey, there goes Kevin." Greg nudged her and Maggie's eyes focused on her son. She cheered as he kicked the ball past the other team's rather bewildered goalie.

"Way to go, Kevin!" shouted the coach, already

hoarse from yelling. He took the game and his team very seriously.

"They're going to win this one!" Maggie cried exultantly.

Greg smiled at her. "You really get into this, don't you?" He remained calm, however, watching the action and applauding any good play, regardless of the team. Unlike some of the fathers present, he didn't upbraid his son when he made a mistake on the playing field. Maggie decided that she admired his sportsmanlike conduct.

The game ended in a victory for Kevin and Josh's team. Kari, Wendy, and Max joined them as they walked toward the Wilders' tan station wagon parked in the blacktop lot. Greg had insisted on driving all of them to the game. "Why don't we go out for lunch?" he suggested, and all five children noisily seconded him. "Where would you like to go? Any suggestions?"

"To Wendy's own place. Wendy's!" Max shouted, and laughed uproariously at his own joke.

Kari liked the idea too. "Wendy wants to go to Wendy's," she said. "And so do I."

"All right. Wendy's it is," agreed Greg.

"Oh, Greg. Greg!" A throaty feminine voice paged Greg from behind. Maggie turned to see a tall slender woman with a glowing tan and a thick mane of blond hair approaching them. She wore well-cut green slacks, a white turtleneck jersey with whales on the collar, and a navy sweater tied around her neck. A trifle overdressed for a children's soccer game, Maggie thought, glancing at her own worn jeans. She watched the woman push her aviator-style sunglasses on top of her head and look admiringly up at Greg.

"I'm so glad I caught you, Greg," the woman purred. Yes, Maggie thought with a grimace, she really did purr like some self-satisfied feline who had just snared a mouse. "I saw you just as we were arriving. Jeremy and Jeffrey's team is playing next."

The woman's voice was attractively breathless. "About tonight . . ."

Maggie was startled, but then thought, of course, it was a Saturday night. Did she think that Greg—Doctor Greg Eligible Wilder—wouldn't have a date? And this chic, sophisticated creature seemed to be it.

"Can you come at seven rather than seven-thirty?" The woman laid her hand on Greg's arm. "You know how hungry children get. I thought we could feed them first and then they could watch a movie while we're . . . eating." A meaningful pause. "I rented *Raiders of the Lost Ark* for the video recorder. That should entertain them, hmm?"

"Are we going to the Smithtons' for dinner tonight, Dad?" Josh asked.

"Yes," the woman answered for Greg, her voice sickeningly sweet. At least it seemed so to Maggie. "Won't that be fun, Josh?" Pure saccharine, Maggie thought. Ugh!

Josh made no reply. Kevin snickered and Maggie stared at her son. She'd never heard him make such a rude, caustic noise in his entire life.

"Taffy, I'd like you to meet the Mays," Greg said smoothly. "Maggie, Kevin, and Kari." He didn't bother to say who was who. "This is Taffy Smithton."

"She's the Smithton twins' mother," said Kevin with a wicked grin.

"Ohh!" breathed Kari.

"It's nice to meet you," Maggie lied. Taffy gave a brief nod, acknowledging the introduction and dismissing Maggie at the same time.

"Looks like the game is about to begin." Greg squinted in the direction of the field. "The kids are all out on the field. We'll, uh, see you tonight, Taffy."

"At seven," she said breezily, giving Greg's arm a friendly little squeeze. "Ciao!"

"Chow?" repeated Max, puzzled.

"She's an old friend," Greg said. He unlocked the doors of the station wagon and the kids piled in. "We used to party with her and her husband."

"Mmm." Maggie feigned indifference. She was aghast at the pangs of jealousy tearing through her. She had guessed, even before Greg added, "They were divorced a year ago," that the woman was unmarried and very much available. Her body language had screamed it.

"You're having dinner with Jeffrey and Jeremy Smithton tonight, Josh," Kevin said, chortling. He began to hum a funeral dirge that had been played as background music on a cartoon show.

"Daddy," Joshua began on a whine, "I don't want to go."

"We have to go. She invited us—all of us—two weeks ago and I accepted." Greg seemed to be addressing Maggie rather than Josh.

"Another date!" Josh complained. "You have too many dates!"

"My mommy doesn't go on dates," Kari announced primly before chiming in with Kevin's funereal drone.

"Stop it, Kevin and Kari!" Maggie snapped, and both children instantly quit humming. She inclined her head slightly toward Greg. "Dr. Wilder, you really don't have to take my children and me to lunch. I know you're busy and—"

"We're going to lunch," Greg said, his jaw clenched. "All of us."

"Turn on the radio," Josh demanded, and Greg immediately flicked it on. The loud rock music accompanied by the children's laughs and shrieks precluded any attempt at conversation during the short drive and Maggie was glad. It was idiotic to feel jealous of the glamorous Taffy, she scolded herself. The only reason Greg had kissed her that morning was because he'd had a womanless, sexless Friday night. A kiss certainly gave her no claims on him, he owed her nothing. Greg Wilder was totally beyond her reach and always would be. How could she have forgotten such a basic fact, even for a little while? Greg's taste in women ran to sophisticated, moneyed beauties like Francine and Taffy. Maggie May was the

sometime baby-sitter for his kids. It was important to
remember their stations in life at all times.

At the restaurant, after they'd gotten their food at
the counter, Greg placed the five children in a booth
in the back. He suggested that he and Maggie sit at a
small table on the opposite side, far from the kids.
She insisted on taking a booth adjoining them. When
she sat down in it, Greg had no choice but to comply.

"I've known Taffy Smithton for years, Maggie," he
said as he squirted ketchup on his french fries. "She
invited us to her place for dinner a month ago."

"Two weeks," she corrected him.

He stared at her, perplexed.

"She invited you and the kids to dinner two
weeks ago," she said sweetly. "That's what you said in
the car earlier."

"She's an old friend of Alicia's, they used to play
bridge together or something." Greg bit viciously into
his cheeseburger. "I used to play golf with her
husband."

"Her ex-husband." Maggie took a dainty bite of
her hamburger. "Greg, you owe me no explanations.
You can go out with whomever you please."

"You're damn right!" he growled. "So don't start
getting possessive on the basis of one kiss."

It had been a lot more than a kiss, Maggie's heart
cried, but her temper quickly overruled such foolish
sentiment. "Me? Possessive of you? Don't flatter
yourself, Greg Wilder. I don't care what you do or who
you do it with." She happened to glance across at the
children then, just in time to see Joshua bury a
packet of french fries in an oozing mound of ketchup.
"That's enough ketchup, Josh," she warned.

"They aren't his french fries, Mommy," Kari
piped up. "They're Wendy's and she hates ketchup."

Maggie looked over at Wendy, who was sitting
back in the seat looking woebegone, tears sliding
down her pale cheeks. "Well, they're Josh's now,"
Maggie said. She reached across the small divider
between the booths and switched the packets of fries,

giving Wendy the plain pack and Josh the over-ketchuped one. Wendy brightened. Joshua scowled.

"Hey, that's not fair!" he said. "Those are Wendy's french fries. I don't like ketchup on mine."

"Too bad. You should have thought of that before you decided to pour it all over Wendy's—who doesn't like ketchup either, as you probably know very well," Maggie said calmly.

"He did it to her hamburger too, Mommy. See?" Kari held up a thoroughly ketchup-laden bun.

"You little tattletale!" Josh doubled his fist and shook it threateningly at Kari. "You're a brat!"

"Sticks and stones may break my bones but names will never hurt me," Kari recited in a singsong chant.

Maggie deftly switched Wendy and Joshua's hamburgers, giving Josh the offending ketchuped one. "All right, Joshua and Kari, that's enough. I don't want to hear another word from either of you. Now eat."

"I can't!" wailed Josh. "I hate ketchup. I won't eat anything with ketchup on it. It'll make me throw up."

"Then don't eat," Maggie said calmly, picking up her own burger and taking a bite.

"I want my hamburger and french fries back!" Josh howled, and made a grab for the hamburger in Wendy's hand. He caught Maggie's eye and abruptly halted in mid-lunge. She continued to stare at him in her most forbidding-mother manner until he settled back in the seat and crossly folded his arms across his chest. Only then did she turn her attention back to her food.

"It isn't fair to take out your anger toward me on the children," Greg said, having observed the scene in silence.

Maggie arched her brows. Evidently he didn't like the sterner side of his sweet Mother Machree image of her. "I'm not angry with you or with the children," she replied coolly. "I simply handled the situation as I thought best."

"And you think it best that my child doesn't eat lunch?" Greg asked in a strained voice. "Josh hates ketchup. He won't eat anything with ketchup on it."

"If he's hungry enough, he'll eat." Maggie reached for a french fry.

"That's an incredibly cold-blooded attitude, Maggie," Greg said, bristling.

"And you thought I was such a saint," she said. "Mother Machree has feet of clay after all."

"Daddy, I'm hungry," Josh complained plaintively. "Can I get a new hamburger and fries? Please, Daddy?"

Greg reached into his pocket and pulled out three one-dollar bills. "The child is hungry," he said to Maggie, his voice defensively sharp. "He spent over an hour running in that soccer game. He needs his food, he's a growing boy!"

"He'll be well on his way to growing into a spoiled brat and a bully if you keep giving in to him this way."

Greg's mouth hardened. "My son is *not* a spoiled brat or a bully," he said indignantly. He handed the money to Joshua with a warm, fatherly smile. "Here you are, Josh. Get some lunch for yourself."

"Thanks, Daddy!" Josh exclaimed. "You're the greatest!"

Greg preened. "You see, he is very appreciative."

"The old soft-soap," Maggie said mockingly. "What's to keep him from dousing Wendy's food with ketchup the next time? Do you intend to keep wasting money on food that no one eats?"

"I can certainly afford the price of one measly hamburger and a pack of fries, Maggie."

"Of course you can, but you're missing the point entirely. Josh is always taking advantage of Wendy. He runs roughshod over her and she never stands up for herself. It was Kari who spoke up for her. Wendy was ready to suffer in silence." Maggie saw Greg set his jaw and knew he didn't like what he was hearing. But she persisted; she couldn't stop now. "What do you think Josh and Wendy learned from this little episode? You've given Josh tacit approval to do whatever he likes to Wendy. She must feel that—"

"Since you don't have a degree in child psychology, I would appreciate it if you skipped the lecture, Maggie. I think I know my own children and I know how to deal with them."

A thousand and one remarks sprang to mind, each one devastatingly sarcastic, but Maggie said nothing. She was smarting too badly over his crack about her lack of a degree. She was very sensitive about her lack of education. She'd wanted to go to college, but in her family a college education was for boys only. She'd married at nineteen as she was supposed to do, become a mother at twenty. And though she had no degree, she did have practical experience with children, a lot of it. Maybe she had spoken out of turn, but she felt on secure ground when it came to children and discipline. She knew her stuff cold in that area, and she simply couldn't sit silently and watch a mistake in the making.

Josh returned to the booth with his new, ketchupless hamburger and french fries and shot Maggie a triumphant look. She didn't react, although she saw Greg frown. They finished their meal in silence. Even the children were subdued. The ride back to Woodland Courts was an abnormally quiet one until Greg stopped the station wagon in front of the Mays' duplex.

"Say thank you to Dr. Wilder for the ride and the lunch," Maggie prompted Kevin and Kari. They obeyed, chorusing their thank yous before running to the front stoop.

" 'Bye, Maggie," called Max. "Will you pick me up at school and bring me here on Monday?"

"I don't know, Max," she replied truthfully. "We'll see." Greg said nothing at all and she wondered if her baby-sitting days for the Wilders were over. It wasn't the first time she had disciplined one of the children, but it was the first time Greg had observed it. And he had made it quite plain that he didn't like the way she had handled the situation.

Max's small face clouded. "It's all your fault, Josh," he accused his brother. "You made Maggie mad and now she doesn't like us anymore."

"That's not true, Max," Maggie said quickly.

"Are you mad at me, Mrs. May?" Josh surprised her by asking.

"No, Josh. But I think you owe your sister an apology."

"I'm sorry, Wendy," he mumbled.

Greg looked as if he'd been poleaxed.

"Will you baby-sit us on Monday after school, Maggie?" asked Wendy in that tiny, little voice of hers.

"That's up to your father, Wendy," Maggie replied.

"Yes," Greg said quickly. He was still reeling from the shock of Joshua's apology to Wendy. When was the last time, if ever, he'd heard that? He turned to Maggie. "Yes, I was just going to ask her, Wendy." Maggie was looking at him, her eyes as cold as green ice. She was going to refuse! he thought. The panic which filled him was way out of proportion to the loss of a baby-sitter. "Please, Maggie?" he added.

She really ought to say no, Maggie thought, and she let Greg read that message in her eyes. But she was terribly fond of the Wilder children and she could certainly use the extra income that caring for them provided. Why disrupt them all simply to get back at Greg? She was neither petty nor vengeful, she told herself loftily. "I'd be happy to keep the kids on Monday," she said. "I'll bring the three of them here after school as usual. Is that all right, Dr. Wilder?"

"Fine," he answered tightly. "I'll pick them up around six-thirty. Don't bother to give them dinner. I'll take them out to eat on our way home."

Maggie nodded briskly and closed the car door. The children called good-bye to her and she waved to them. Then she turned and walked to her front door where Kevin and Kari awaited her.

"Boy, are they ever in for a night tonight!" Kevin said with a gleeful grin. "The Smithton twins! They're awful! Kari and I saw them get thrown out of the library for tearing up the books and spitting on the library lady. She said they can never come back. They aren't allowed in the Community Center either."

"They don't go to Woodland School, do they?" Maggie asked. She couldn't recall seeing their names on the school roster. And such a pair would definitely be well known to the office personnel who had to usher young offenders into the principal's office. The Smithton twins sounded like they'd be regulars.

"Nope, they go to some special school for wild maniacs," Kevin told her with relish.

"The Eastern Hills School?" Maggie had heard of the private school in Baltimore for children with severe behavioral problems. Many of its students had been kicked out of the public school system for disciplinary reasons. It was rumored that the Eastern Hills teachers were given combat pay.

"The library lady said they're the worst boys in town," Kari said. "Maybe in the whole world," she added dramatically. "Poor Wendy!"

"Poor Josh," chimed in Kevin. "And poor Max and poor Dr. Wilder."

"Yes." Maggie smiled with pure malice. "Poor, *poor* Dr. Wilder."

Four

Early Sunday afternoon, Greg pulled his car up in front of the Mays', turned off the engine, and sat staring at the small duplex. He wasn't sure why he was there, or what excuse he would give Maggie if she asked. He only knew that he had to see her. He'd lain awake until the early hours of the morning trying to understand his sudden obsession with Maggie. When had she become so important to him?

Although Josh had been a friend of Kevin May, and Alicia had known Maggie casually for a few years, he hadn't met Maggie himself until the day before Alicia's funeral. She had appeared at the door of his house with a coffee cake, which one of Alicia's many woman friends had taken away to the kitchen. He had been in a state of shock, numbed by the sudden death of his wife and dazed by the tranquilizers forced on him by his fellow physicians. Nevertheless, he remembered Maggie and her coffee cake well. She had offered to watch Max the next day, the day of Alicia's funeral, and Greg had been grateful. Alicia had many friends, all of whom wanted to attend her funeral rather than spend the day with her two-year-old son. Alicia's parents weren't up to coping with their youngest grandchild either; they were too devastated by their daughter's death. So it had been agreed that Maggie would come for Max and keep him at her

house the day of the funeral. In the end, she'd taken
Josh and Wendy too. Greg had given them the option
of attending the funeral and they had opted out.

The memory of that day was hazy, yet he remembered parts of it with crystal clarity. One part he
clearly remembered was driving to 909 Woodland
Courts late that night to pick up his three younger
children. The children were fine, Maggie had assured
him. They'd spent the day playing. Little Max had
napped and all three had eaten well. She thought it
was wise of him not to have forced Josh and Wendy to
attend the funeral services. She hadn't taken her
Kristin to Johnny's funeral either. Greg had been
grateful for the supporting words. Alicia's parents
and most of her friends had told him that Josh and
Wendy ought to have been present. No, Maggie had
said, not if they didn't want to go. He had been right
and should pay no attention to what other people
said.

He had offered to pay her and she'd refused,
insisting that her services were those of a friend for a
friend, Kevin's mother for Joshua's father. But if he
ever needed a baby-sitter for the children in the
future, she would be happy to take the job and let him
pay her for it, she'd informed him with a soft smile.

The arrangements made for the children's care
had been rather chaotic in the following months, and
Maggie May had been one of many sitters he'd used.
But within the past year he had used her almost
exclusively. Paula was developing an active social life
and wasn't always available to stay with her younger
sister and brothers. And the combination of his
demanding profession and his own frenzied social life
required many hours of baby-sitting services. It was
convenient and easy to call Maggie. She was
extremely competent and never refused and he knew
she needed the money. The kids liked her and were
happy with her; her children were their best friends.
She was always smiling and pleasant when she
greeted him at the door, always had some humorous

little story or joke that made him smile. He'd found himself looking forward to seeing her at the end of his working day. She always managed to give his spirits a lift.

It had only been within the last few months that he'd realized he had never been inside her home. Each time he arrived to pick up the children, he wondered if this would be the day he would make it inside. It had become sort of a private joke, but on Friday night the joke had abruptly ceased to be funny.

Had it begun that night, this urgency, this *need* to be with her? When Francine had dropped her facade of sexy compliance to reveal the shrew within, he hadn't been able to help comparing her appalling behavior toward Max with Maggie's kindness and caring. And yesterday morning when he had seen Maggie in her nightgown, looking tousled and sleepy and incredibly appealing, he had instantly imagined her waking in his bed, looking like that. He'd pictured himself reaching for her, taking her . . . And he had seen in her eyes, those beautiful green eyes, that she was aware of him too. She was finally seeing him as a man and not as the Wilder children's daddy. Greg could never remember wanting to touch a woman as badly as he had wanted to touch her on that narrow staircase. She'd managed to wipe all thoughts of Alicia from his mind, something that had never happened before. It was Maggie, only Maggie, who he'd wanted, and *nothing* could have stopped him from taking her in his arms. Her explosive reaction to his kiss had fired a passion within him that he had thought long dead. For the first time since Alicia's death his emotions as well as his physical urges had been involved. He had wanted to make love to Maggie until they were both exhausted and insensible, and then to make love to her again. But of course that hadn't happened. Reality, in the form of their children, had intervened.

A relationship with Maggie could only be fraught with complications, frustrations, and irritations.

They had seven children between them, an awesome thought! It was best that he overcome this infatuation, or whatever it was, very soon. He could have—and did have—physical relations with women who were just as attractive as Mary Magdalene May. More attractive! And without those pint-sized confusions and interruptions. But here he was, sitting in his car in front of her house like a nervous teenager on a first date, impossibly eager to see her, to touch her, again.

"Mom! It's for you!" Kevin bellowed into the mouthpiece of the phone. Whoever was on the other end of the line would have a nasty case of reverberating eardrums.

Maggie handed eighteen-month-old Nicole Chiarelli to Kristin and took the phone, glancing at the clock on the wall. Kevin spoke up, as if on cue. "I'm hungry, Mom. When's lunch?"

"You can fix yourself a bologna and cheese sandwich now, if you want," she said to him, then turned her attention to the caller on the phone. "Hello?"

"Maggie? This is Rich Cassidy. From school."

"Of course. How are you, Rich?" Rich Cassidy was the music director at Woodland, in charge of both the elementary and junior high school bands. She'd met him when he had come into the school office and had talked with him several times.

They exchanged the usual, general pleasantries, then Rich said, "I've located a used trumpet, Maggie. I wondered if you were still interested in it for your son? I start giving the fourth-graders lessons on their instruments next month."

Maggie vaguely recalled discussing instruments and Kevin and music lessons with Rich Cassidy one day in the office. Had she actually told him that Kevin wanted to play the trumpet? She grimaced. She was just being polite, if not entirely truthful, during that conversation. Kevin had never mentioned wanting to play an instrument to her.

"The previous owner is willing to sell the trumpet for forty dollars, which anyone familiar with instruments will tell you is an absolute steal. It's in mint condition. And, of course, the music lessons at school are free. Are you interested, Maggie?"

"Just a minute, Rich." She put her hand over the mouthpiece and whispered to Kevin, "Do you want to play the trumpet?"

Kevin amazed her by replying enthusiastically, "Oh, boy, yeah!"

She smiled weakly. "We'll take the trumpet, Rich." Mentally calculating the cost, she decided they could afford the forty dollars. She had little Nicole today from six to six and that would net over thirty dollars at her fee of three dollars per hour. And tomorrow, Monday, she had the Wilder children for several hours.

"Great!" Rich said. "And, uh, Maggie . . . I was wondering if you would like to go to a concert with me this coming Saturday?"

He sounded so unsure of himself, yet so hopeful. Had he tracked down the used trumpet as an excuse to call her in the first place? Maggie wondered. She felt a pang of empathy for the man. One of her brothers had been quite shy and she understood the effort it must have taken to make this call. "This coming Saturday?" she repeated. He'd called nearly a full week in advance. How flattering, she thought warmly.

"Yes. The concert begins at seven-thirty," Rich said hopefully.

"I'd like to go," Maggie heard herself saying. And then the facts dawned. He'd asked her for a date and she had accepted. It would be the first date she'd had since she'd been widowed six years ago.

"Great!" Rich said again. They talked about the weather for a few minutes before hanging up.

Maggie pondered the situation as she made lunch for the children. Little Nicole sat in Kari's old high chair, entrancing the girls with her toddler's antics.

"I wish we had a baby sister," Kari said, sighing longingly as Nicole overturned a bowl and put it on her head.

"Me too," Kristin echoed. "I'd even settle for a baby brother."

"You need a dad for that," Kevin informed them with nine-year-old wisdom. "And we don't have one."

"If Mommy got married again we would," Kristin said, "And maybe they'd have a new baby. Wouldn't that be great?"

"I'd rather have the new dad than the new baby," Kevin decided.

Maggie smiled absently, not really listening, lost in her own thoughts. She was still surprised that she'd accepted Rich Cassidy's invitation without a moment's hesitation. In the past she'd turned down the occasional offer of a date quickly and firmly, slightly scandalized that anyone had dared to ask. She was a mother, not a date! And she had felt very much married to Johnny for a long time after his death. But gradually she had begun to accept her widowed status. Today's yes to Rich seemed to signify the completion of the process.

Inevitably, her thoughts turned to Greg and their hot kisses on the staircase the day before. Perhaps *that* was the episode that had signified her acknowledgment of her single woman status. She hadn't thought of Johnny *or* the children then! Her whole body felt warm at the memory.

She still had trouble believing it had actually happened. She had been baby-sitting for his children steadily for the past two years, but Greg had never before touched her or even indicated that he wanted to. She doubted that he'd even thought of her as a woman. Oh, she knew he liked her as a person. When they chatted together in the doorway, his eyes were warm and friendly and he always laughed at her jokes. But yesterday he had looked at her in a whole new way. He had kissed her and touched her . . . intimately. Maggie felt a tightening in her midsection and recognized the sensation as one long-forgotten but unexpectedly revived by Greg. It was sexual arousal.

Had she unconsciously given some sort of signal to indicate that she was no longer strictly a mother but a woman as well? Had Rich Cassidy picked up on that message too? Maggie remembered reading that a woman's body came into its sexual prime in the years past thirty, and the implications scared her. She wasn't about to start in on a mad sexual whirl, sleeping her way from Baltimore to Washington with any man who came along, no matter what her body thought it craved! She had three children and a stable family life and old-fashioned morals, and she would have to get *that* message across to Rich Cassidy . . . and Greg Wilder. She reminded herself that he'd had a date last night and that Taffy had plans for him while the children were tucked away in front of the video recorder.

Maggie sliced the dill pickle with unaccustomed zeal. She hoped the Smithton twins had reached new lows in terrorist behavior. She recalled her frozen parting with Greg the previous afternoon and slashed the pickle harder.

"Mommy, you cut it into a zillion pieces," Kari said, pointing at the hacked-up pickle. "It looks yucky. I don't want any."

"You don't have to have any, honey," Maggie said sweetly. "Kevin will eat it." Kevin ate anything.

"Kids, how would you feel about me going to a concert on Saturday with Mr. Cassidy?" she asked. She decided it was only fair to solicit the children's opinions. If they were adamantly opposed to her going out, she would of course change her plans. The kids came first in her life. If they didn't want her to leave them . . .

"Like on a date?" Kevin asked, wide-eyed.

"Um, yes," Maggie said.

"Can we still watch TV that night?" Kari asked.

"Of course. Kristin can baby-sit. It will only be for a few hours and she *is* in junior high now. Or, if you prefer, I'll ask Mrs. Jenkins to come over and stay with you."

"Just the three of us here by ourselves?" Kevin's blue eyes sparkled with enthusiasm. "Oh, boy!"

"I'd be happy to baby-sit, Mom," Kristin said. "You go out on your date. We'll be fine." She grinned at her brother and sister.

"Are you sure?" Maggie looked at Kari.

"Sure," replied her baby. "Go, Mommy. Have fun."

The sound of the doorbell precluded any further discussion, not that any more was needed. The children had given their unanimous approval. Maggie was wiping the baby's face and hands with a wet cloth when she heard Kristin say deferentially, "Hi, Dr. Wilder. Come on in."

Maggie froze and nearly dropped little Nicole. Greg!

"Oh, goody, Wendy is here," cried Kari, rushing from the kitchen. Kevin followed her.

And then she heard Greg's voice. "No, I didn't bring the kids. Paula is staying with them. Where's your mother?"

Greg without the children? Maggie hoisted little Nicole onto her hip and joined Greg and her children in the cramped entranceway. Although the kids had changed from their "Sunday best" into jeans and sweatshirts, she still wore her silky, long-sleeved kelly green shirtwaist dress. Her auburn hair, clean and shiny, swung against her neck in its smooth pageboy style. Just as she was about to greet Greg, little Nicole grabbed one of her gold hoop earrings, held on tight, and pulled.

"Ouch! No, no, Nicky!" Maggie caught the baby's hand and carefully uncurled the little fingers from around the earring. It was not the entrance she would have wished to make.

"Hello, Maggie," Greg said, his eyes widening slightly. "Where did the baby come from?" He sounded like his old friendly self. Were yesterday's arguments—and kisses—forgotten?

"From the cabbage patch," Maggie said, resuming her old role, complete with light banter. Greg responded with his customary chuckle. The kids giggled. "This is Nicole," she explained. "We have her from six to six today and the girls are in seventh heaven." She was pleased to hear herself sounding just like her usual efficient baby-sitter/mother self.

"You're baby-sitting today? On Sunday? From six to six?" Greg fired the questions at her. Curiously, a look of annoyance crossed his face. "Do you ever *not* work?"

"Not as long as my kids and I want to eat," she replied lightly. It wasn't really that desperate. Johnny's policeman's death benefits were ample and there was social security for the children as well. But Maggie wanted much more for her children. She wanted them to have nice clothes and whatever lessons they wanted to take and special toys and, most of all, a college education. For her son and both her daughters. So she held a full-time, though not high-paying, job and baby-sat in her spare hours.

"What can we do for you today, Dr. Wilder?" She deliberately made her tone briskly impersonal. What *was* he doing here?

Greg was again wondering the same thing. Some compulsion that he couldn't begin to understand, much less explain, had caused him to leave Paula with the younger children and drive to Woodland Courts. Although Kristin had immediately invited him inside when she'd answered the door, Maggie had clearly resumed her role in their previous superficial, impersonal doorstep relationship. What *was* he doing here?

"Well, I thought I would—" he began, only to be interrupted by Kari.

"Mommy, can I take Nicole upstairs to my room?"

she asked. She was clearly bored by the adults' company. Nicole was bored too; she was making wild grabs for Maggie's earrings. Maggie handed the baby to Kari.

"She balances her on her hip just the way you do," Greg observed, smiling at Maggie in spite of himself. It was a cute sight, Kari carrying little Nicole that way. Maggie smiled too.

"Mom, call me when Jennifer gets here. She said she was coming over after lunch," Kristin called over her shoulder as she followed Kari up the stairs.

"I'm going out to play now, Mom," Kevin announced on his way out the door. " 'Bye!" The door slammed shut, leaving Greg and Maggie alone.

"It's always incredibly busy around here," Greg said with a slight smile.

Maggie nodded, too intensely aware of him to respond with the bright chatter that the situation demanded. Today he was wearing a well-cut pair of khaki slacks, a blue oxford cloth shirt, and a navy windbreaker, casual clothes which complemented his muscular physique. She wished again for that distancing note of animosity they had parted on the day before. It was easier to handle her attraction to him when she was angry with him.

"I was in the, uh, neighborhood—I stopped in at the drugstore—and I thought I would . . ." Greg swallowed, his eyes focusing on the soft curve of her mouth. "I thought I'd drop by and finalize the baby-sitting arrangements for tomorrow."

"I'm to take Josh and Wendy with me after school, pick up Max at the day-care center, and bring all of them here. You'll pick them up at six-thirty and I'm not to give them dinner," Maggie said automatically.

"Er—yes. I believe those were the arrangements." Greg thrust his hands deep into the pockets of his slacks. "Oh, hell, that isn't the real reason why I came over."

"Oh?" Maggie felt a ridiculous surge of anticipation. He was staring fixedly at her, a strange expression in his clear blue eyes. She wasn't exactly sure how to define it. Uncertainty, confusion, surprise? As she returned his gaze, she realized her lips were parted and trembling, that every nerve in her body was blazing with sensual awareness. She heard the sounds of the girls playing upstairs, Nicole's pleased squeals, Kari and Kristin's laughter, but they seemed far away and irrelevant to the flames shooting through her.

"Maggie." Greg said her name in a low, husky voice. He took a step toward her and she didn't move. Her eyes were focused on his mouth with a hunger that hurt. They seemed to be caught in some strange, silent time warp, just the two of them, far removed from the rest of the everyday world.

Greg was standing so close to her now that she could feel his body heat, inhale his heady masculine scent. Her heart seemed to be crashing against her rib cage as she lifted her eyes to his. She was aching to touch him. She wanted to feel his mouth on hers with an intensity that shook her to her core.

"Come here," he said hoarsely, reaching for her, pulling her roughly, urgently, into his arms. Maggie felt the solid hardness of his chest against her breasts and her body melted into his, shuddering with an intense pleasure: "I have to hold you, Maggie. I can't look at you without wanting to touch you, feel you . . ." His voice trailed off as he slowly lowered his head to hers. Their mouths met and they kissed with a wild, desperate urgency, as if starved for the touch and feel and taste of each other.

His big hands caressed her, moving greedily over her hips and waist and back. When he took possession of her breasts, cupping and kneading them with his palms, Maggie moaned with the mad hunger that was coursing through her body. He pulled her closer, bending her back slightly so that her body fit beneath his, and she had to cling to him for support. She was dizzy with the sensations and emotions pulsing through her. The feel of his strong shoulders and powerful chest beneath her fingertips excited her as much as his passionate caresses. His tongue surged into her mouth, and she met it and rubbed it with her own. A moan escaped simultaneously from each of their throats and the kiss deepened, becoming more demanding, more intimate.

The insistent, incessant pounding seemed to come from another dimension. At first Maggie thought it was her own heartbeat thundering in her ears; then she thought it was Greg's. It wasn't until the shrill ring of the doorbell shattered the sensual silence of their private world that Maggie recognized the sound for what it really was. Someone was pounding on the front door and alternately ringing the bell. She broke away from Greg, her face flushed and her body shaking with arousal and unmet needs. As she rushed to the door, Greg walked in the opposite direction, into the kitchen.

"Hi, Mrs. May," Jennifer greeted her cheerily. "Kristin here?" She was looking past Maggie toward the stairs where the children's voices drifted downward.

Maggie was grateful for a child's typical lack of interest in an adult. Jennifer was looking for her friend and had scarcely glanced at Maggie. Why should she? Thank heavens, Maggie thought, her tousled hair and flushed face and slightly swollen lips weren't even noticed by Jennifer.

"Go on up, Jennifer. Nicole is with them. We're baby-sitting for her all day." Maggie smoothed her hair with nervous fingers. Her knees were trembling so much that she was amazed she was able to stand. Jennifer raced up the stairs, taking two steps at a time.

"Another kid," Greg said as he rejoined her at the door. "Just what you need around here." His pupils were still dilated with passion and his mouth was tight and fixed. Maggie's eyes dropped inadvertently to his belt buckle and the straining masculinity below. She blushed. "Yes." Greg grimaced wryly as his eyes followed the direction of hers. "What are we going to do about that, Maggie?"

She said nothing, wanting desperately to toss off some glib and flippant remark. Now was certainly the time for it. But she couldn't. She'd never been able to make light of her deepest emotions.

"Maggie, will you go for a drive with me? I want to be alone with you and there's not a chance of it here."

What was he really asking? she wondered confusedly. Did he want to go for a drive and talk, or would they drive to some motel and seek a quick release for their pent-up frustrations? It seemed likely that he meant the latter. They could certainly talk here, couldn't they? Maggie burned at the thought, feeling shamefully wanton and horribly confused. "No!" She sounded more harsh than she'd intended and Greg frowned.

"Why not?" he asked. "Can't Kristin and her friend stay with the little ones for a while?"

"I think we had this same conversation yesterday." Maggie was slowly recovering her wits, sanity was returning. She thought of the tempestuous Francine and Greg's urgency the day before; she remembered the chic Taffy and Greg's urgency today. "Struck out with Cookie last night, did you?" She couldn't bring herself to say the woman's name aloud. It was bad enough being a stand-in for an adult named Taffy.

Greg looked puzzled for a moment, then his scowl deepened. "Do you mean Taffy? Taffy Smithton?"

"Whatever. I knew it had something to do with sugar." Maggie set her jaw and eyed him defiantly. "I'm just as averse to being used as an outlet for your frustration today as I was yesterday."

"Meaning what?" Greg snapped.

"Meaning that you didn't make it to bed with—with your date last night either. It shows, Greg."

"Ah, yes, your theory. Now I remember. And so, according to your insightful premise, I've gone a whole weekend without sex and am now a raving maniac, ready to accost anything in a skirt. Why else would I want you?"

Put that way, it sounded terribly crass and unflattering. Maggie felt a hot flush crawl up her body.

"And you, of course, being a hot, sex-starved widow, are hungry for any male body that happens to come your way. Why don't I just shove you against the wall and give it to you, Maggie? That should satisfy both of us sex-crazed animals."

He was furious with her, and some calm, detached part of him recognized the conversion of his passion into anger. While he'd tossed and turned the night before, his racing thoughts came to rest inevitably, obsessively, on Maggie May. Her physical effect upon him was stunning, and so totally unexpected that he still couldn't quite fathom it. Why? he wondered rather desperately. How?

"All right," Maggie said, interrupting his thoughts, "I—I shouldn't have implied that you're a sex-crazed animal." She wondered what was going on in Greg's mind. She saw a range of emotions playing across his face, watched his eyes alternately lighten and darken as he thought, but he remained a complete enigma to her. "I don't appreciate the allusion myself." She smiled suddenly, disarming him completely. "By the way, how *was* your evening with Mrs. Smithton and her, uh, boys?"

"You knew! You knew about those two psychopaths and you didn't even warn me!"

"I didn't know until Kevin told me about them, after you'd already left." Greg looked so disgruntled, Maggie couldn't help grinning. "And you said you were old friends. I assumed you knew the boys as well as their mother."

"Believe me, Taffy keeps them under wraps and with good reason. Alicia and I knew Taffy and Jack Smithton casually, but we'd never gotten together with our families. If we had, I would have known not to come within ten miles of those twin monsters."

"So you didn't have a good time?" Maggie asked with false sympathy, her green eyes glowing with glee.

"A good time?" he repeated incredulously. "Let's put it this way, I'd rather repeat my entire neurosurgery residency than ever spend another hour with those two little fiends. I can clearly see prison in their future and I'm not a shade psychic."

She laughed and a moment later he joined her. "It's been one hell of a weekend," he said, smiling ruefully. "The only good parts have been with you."

Maggie's heart lurched. She wanted to believe him, yet was too uncertain to do it. Greg was an experienced man. He could have any woman he wanted and it seemed doubtful that he would want a woman as average and as ordinary as she. Oh, she didn't doubt that she and her children fared better in his estimation than did the Smithton horrors. Who wouldn't? So she must not read too much into his words. Why would a man with as much to offer a woman as Greg want to become involved with a financially strapped widow with three young children? He had four children of his own to contend with. Why, between them they had seven children, quite an awesome thought!

There was the sound of footsteps and children's voices on the stairs, and Kristin, Kari, and Jennifer appeared with little Nicole perched on Kristin's hip. "Can we take Nicole for a walk, Mom?" Kristin asked.

Maggie nodded. "But stay within the block, girls. I want to put the baby down for her nap in about half an hour."

Greg and Maggie watched the noisy little group depart. "I wish Paula was as crazy about little ones as your girls seem to be," Greg said, then sighed. "I'm afraid I've overused her as a baby-sitter. Today she told me that she never wants to have kids when she grows up, that they're too much trouble and take up all of your time and are no fun."

"I wouldn't take her too seriously, Greg. It's just her age. I'm sure there isn't a teenage baby-sitter alive who hasn't had those feelings at least once."

"Really? You know a lot about kids and their feelings, Maggie."

"Mmm. And their tricks as well. That's because I was a rotten little kid who tried everything. My mother tells me I don't deserve Kristin, Kevin, and Kari. After what I put her and Daddy through as a kid, she feels I deserve children like—like the Smithton twins."

"Oh, please, don't mention those demons. It was really a terrible night, Maggie. Those two brats bullied Max and teased Wendy and inspired Josh to new levels of obnoxiousness. He poured a whole bottle of ketchup on poor Wendy's hot dog. A whole bottle!"

"Uh-oh. What happened next?"

"I made him eat the whole damn hot dog, every bite." Greg's eyes gleamed as he caught her look of surprise. "Like I should have done at lunch yesterday. On the way home from the Smithtons' Josh told me that he would never dump ketchup on Wendy's food again because he knew he'd have to eat it."

"I think that's called behavioral reinforcement." She smiled. "But, of course, I'm no psychologist."

Greg put his hands on her shoulders, his fingers curving gently to cup them. "Maybe not. But you *are* a perceptive and very wise woman, sweet Maggie."

They stood smiling at each other and it seemed the most natural thing in the world for him to take her into his arms. Or did she move into them of her own accord? Perhaps, Maggie thought, they moved toward each other simultaneously. She wasn't sure, but she was sure of the happiness and warm sense of rightness she felt when Greg's lips met hers. They shared a long, tender kiss that quickly flamed into passion and left them clinging and caressing, the only two people in their own private world.

Except they weren't. A door slammed and there was the sound of footsteps and a sudden, stunned "Yow!"

Maggie pulled free and whirled to face Kevin, who had come running in through the back door. She was horrified by her distinctly unmaternal desire at that moment to tell her only son to get lost.

"Mom!" Kevin was obviously awed. "You were kissing Dr. Wilder!"

Maggie first felt icy cold, then scalded. "Kevin, I—" she began at the same time that Greg said in a shaky voice, "Kevin, we—"

They both lapsed into silence, staring at Kevin and carefully avoiding each other's eyes. Kevin didn't seem unduly traumatized by the sight of his mother kissing his best friend's father. He looked interested. "Are you going to go out on a date with Dr. Wilder, Mom?" he asked.

How did one explain such a situation to a nine-year-old? Maggie wondered frantically. Especially when she barely understood it herself. She took a deep breath. "No, Kevin."

"Yes, Kevin," Greg said at the same time. "Yes, she is."

Kevin looked pleased. "My mom is sure getting a lot of dates lately."

"Kevin!" Maggie's voice rose on a warning note.

"Is she?" Greg's voice was silky. "A lot of dates, you say, Kevin?"

"Yeah." Kevin nodded.

"Kevin, go back out and play, honey," Maggie said sweetly.

"I came in to get a drink. Can I have some juice, Mom?"

"Of course." She resisted the urge to shove him into the kitchen. "Of course, darling."

"Can Timmy and Bill and Joey and Matt come in and have some too? We're awfully thirsty, Mom. And hungry. Can we have some cookies?"

The little blackmailer, Maggie thought grimly.

She inhaled deeply and cast a covert glance at Greg. He was tense and unsmiling. "Yes, Kevin, you can bring your friends in for juice and cookies. But use paper cups and stay in the kitchen."

"We will. Thanks, Mom!" Kevin was gone in a flash.

"What did he mean, a lot of dates lately?" Greg demanded the moment the child had left the room. "I thought Kari said you didn't date at all."

"Oh, I don't." Maggie laughed nervously. Until a few hours ago, Kari had been right. "You know how children—especially little boys—love to exaggerate."

Greg frowned. "I want you to go out with me on Saturday night, Maggie. We'll go to dinner and a movie or dancing, anything you want."

"I, uh, can't, Greg."

"Why not?"

She gulped. "I, er, already have a date for Saturday."

"Ha! I suspected it! Kevin wasn't exaggerating at all. So you've suddenly decided to begin dating again, hmm?" His voice lowered to a soft deadliness. "With whom do you have this . . . date on Saturday, Maggie?"

It was ridiculous to feel so nervous, so guilty, she scolded herself. The mental pep talk didn't work though. She still felt nervous and guilty, as if she were somehow being unfaithful to Greg. Which really *was* an absurd notion, she thought. How many times had she stayed with his children while he went out with assorted and sundry women? Enough times to pay her electric bill several months running!

"Who is it, Maggie?"

"Someone named Rich Cassidy. You probably don't know him," she added hopefully.

"Rich Cassidy? Is he the twerp who gives music lessons at school? The director of the elementary and junior high school bands?"

Maggie managed a weak smile. "I guess you do know him."

"Oh, yes, I know him. And I detest the little creep! He kicked Paula out of the junior high band last year. She was the best flute player they had and Cassidy had the nerve to kick her out!"

Maggie stared at him. Were there actually words one could use in a situation like this? If so, she certainly couldn't think of them. "Why did he kick Paula out of the band?" she managed at last.

"She missed a few of his stupid band practices. Not that she even needed to be there. She was better than anyone else in the whole damn band. But Cassidy has this asinine rule about not missing more than five practices without being absent from school and . . ." His voice trailed off. "I don't want to discuss it any further. And I don't want you to go out with him, Maggie."

"Because he kicked Paula out of the band?"

"Don't be flippant, Maggie. I don't like it."

"And I don't like it when you try to tell me who I should or shouldn't go out with," she said, her temper starting to flare.

"I'm not trying to tell you, I *am* telling you. You're not going out with Cassidy or anyone else. The only man you're permitted to date is me!"

"Permitted?" She had never heard Greg use that insufferably domineering tone before. No man used that tone to her! Her older brothers had never used it, nor had Johnny May and, most certainly, she would not let Greg Wilder talk to her that way.

"Don't start getting possessive on the basis of a few kisses." She threw his offensive jibe of the day before back in his face with pleasure. "I'll go out with whoever I please."

"The hell you will!" He grabbed her arms and pulled her roughly against him. "I won't let you play these games with me! You're—you're mine!" He swore savagely and his mouth swooped down on hers in an audaciously possessive kiss.

She should be fighting him, Maggie thought dizzily. She should be pushing him away with both hands, rejecting this male display of territorial dominance. But the impact of his body against hers, the touch of his hands, the hard pressure of his mouth, dissolved her resistance and her outrage was swiftly converted into a thoroughly intoxicating passion. Every time he touched her, her responses came more rapidly and were more intense. She clutched at him, her senses spinning, and arched her body against his, claiming his mouth for her own in an equally proprietary way.

They kissed fiercely, deeply, with a possessive and passionate hunger that consumed them both. Greg thrust his burgeoning manhood against the soft feminine cradle of her thighs. She moaned and tried to press even closer, to fit herself to him, wanting him with a wild urgency that she had never before experienced. She felt completely, excitingly, out of control, every nerve focused on the throbbing, aching void that demanded to be filled. By Greg. Only he could complete her. Maggie whispered his name in soft, pleading wonder.

Their clothing had become an intolerable barrier that she longed to rip away. She was having difficulty standing up. She wanted to lie down with Greg in her arms, wanted to feel his skin touching hers. To explore him, every inch of him, to feel him deep inside her.

Kevin and his friends suddenly came banging through the back door into the kitchen. The refrigerator door opened and closed a dozen times, cabinet doors slammed, ice cubes rattled, paper rustled. The presence of the exuberantly loud small boys brought Greg and Maggie's crazily passionate, reckless interlude to an abrupt end. Greg released his hold on her just as she started to move away from him. Their eyes locked, their faces flushed and breathing erratic.

"Now look what you did, you dope! You spilled it!" came an incriminating bellow from the kitchen. "It wasn't me, it was Joey!" was the indignant reply.

"Hey, Bill's grabbing all the big cookies!" "Gimme that!" "Uh-oh!"

Maggie forced herself out of her sensual trance. She was trembling, her eyes glazed as she headed automatically toward the fracas in the kitchen. "I'll see you tomorrow, Greg," she said softly, her voice husky and thick. She loved the sound of his name on her lips. "When you come to pick up the children." His adorable children whom she dearly loved.

Greg made no reply. A few seconds later, as she reached for the mop to clean up the disaster in her kitchen, Maggie heard the front door slam shut and she knew he was gone.

Five

Maggie dreamed of Greg that night. When she awoke Monday morning, she felt tense and highstrung and in the throes of a delicious, feverish excitement. The emotional high persisted throughout the day. She somehow performed competently at work, typing, Xeroxing, answering the switchboard, and dealing with the numerous routine and unexpected events inevitable in an elementary school with some eight hundred children.

But her thoughts consistently returned to Greg. His face seemed to be continually in her mind's eye, as if the man had been imprinted on her brain. She saw him at the soccer match applauding and encouraging all the young players. She saw him hugging Max and holding Wendy on his lap and discussing the gymnastic meet with Kristin. Her lips curved into a smile as she remembered his vexed frown when she and Max had teased him about a spanking. And she almost chuckled aloud when she recalled his appalled expression as he'd related his miserable evening with the dreadful Smithton twins.

And then there were the other, more disturbing, memories. The passion in his gorgeous aquamarine eyes moments before he claimed her mouth with his. His voice, husky and deep, as he reached for her. "Come here . . . I have to hold you . . ."

And, of course, there was that wild, passionate quarrel. Greg had been jealous, she thought, thrilled. Again and again she relived that quarrel and it seemed to become more exciting and dynamic each time. First the angry words, then Greg's fiercely possessive "You're mine!" as he yanked her into his arms. And then that incredibly passionate kiss which had left her reeling. The force of her own desire rocked her. She couldn't remember ever feeling such devastating urgency, such want and need. Never! She hadn't even believed such feelings existed, in her or in anyone else. She'd read all about being overwhelmed by passion but thought it simply a media invention. Something to sell books and magazines, to bring people into the theaters. Certainly nothing to do with real people and real lives.

Her relationship with Greg was making her reassess her previous beliefs which had been based, after all, on her own experiences in life. She had loved Johnny May dearly, but from a distance of six long years she was now able to view their physical relationship somewhat objectively. She'd been a girl when she'd married, just nineteen years old, and she had become pregnant with Kristin two short months later. With Johnny she had experienced the loving closeness of the sexual act, but never the explosive pleasure she'd read about. Because, she had decided, it didn't exist. It was simply a myth some people wrote about and other people read about, but nobody actually experienced. Woe to the poor fools who thought they were missing something in their rather bland and routine relations and tried to find the mythical sexual nirvana. Maggie had been proud that she'd discovered this secret so young. There would be no foolish longing for her! She accepted what she had and told herself it was everything she wanted. Of course she didn't share her revelation with Johnny. She loved him and he seemed perfectly satisfied with her in bed. She knew he loved her too. She suspected that Johnny already knew what she had learned about sex. He never expected fireworks either. Their sexual relationship very quickly took a back seat to the demands of their babies and Johnny's ever-changing work hours. As a policeman he'd worked all three shifts at different times. He had been a good husband, loyal and affectionate, but not at all sexually demanding. Neither of the Mays had minded going weeks without sex.

Maggie's thoughts drifted from the past to the present. She already knew that Greg Wilder was a very different type of man from Johnny. He was hot-headed, more physical, more demanding and—she swallowed—far more sexually experienced than Johnny had been. She could tell by the way he kissed, by his sure, confident caresses. And his physical relationship with his wife must have differed drastically from hers with Johnny. Greg wouldn't be satisfied with a quick good-night kiss on the cheek for weeks on end, as Johnny had been. The thought both excited and depressed her and she wondered why.

At three-thirty, Kevin and Kari and Josh and Wendy all gathered in the school office and Maggie drove them to the Woodland Children's Center where Max spent his days—mornings in the preschool program and afternoons in day care. She took all five children to the duplex where they awaited the arrival of Kristin fifteen minutes later. All six kids had the traditional after-school snack of milk and cookies in the kitchen and then went outside to play. Homework at the Mays' was done after dinner, before there could be any thought of watching television. Maggie didn't know when homework was done at the Wilders. From overhearing Josh and Kevin's talk of Josh's marks, probably not at all.

She made chili for dinner and decided that when Greg arrived to pick up the children, she would tell him that she'd changed her mind about going to the concert with Rich Cassidy on Saturday. What was the point of going? She wasn't interested in dating per se. The only man she wanted to be with was Greg Wilder. She would tell him tonight that she was free on Saturday. She sighed dreamily as she stirred the red kidney beans into the chili. "I want you to go out with me on Saturday night," Greg had said in that rather thrilling, masterful voice. Well, she was going to do just that.

Six-thirty came and went. Josh had already eaten a bowl of chili, along with the Mays—he was too starved to wait for his dinner, he'd pleaded. Wendy and Max refused the chili but eagerly accepted the alphabet soup and crackers Maggie offered them. And everyone had a piece of chocolate cake and a glass of milk. She could hardly deny hungry children something to eat, Maggie thought sympathetically as she doled out the food. Greg would understand why she had ignored his instructions not to feed the kids any dinner.

At ten minutes to seven the doorbell rang and Maggie had to restrain herself from racing madly to answer it. Smoothing her palms over the pleats in her gray skirt, she forced herself to walk to the door and greet Greg with a calm smile. Beneath her cool exterior her heart was pounding wildly and butterflies seemed to be rioting in her stomach.

"Hello, Greg," she said. She was proud that her voice sounded so normal. She was so glad to see him that she wanted to fling herself into his arms. But she was too uncertain, still too shy of him and their new tempestuous relationship, to make the first move. That would have to come from Greg. She clutched the screen door and tried to keep herself on an even keel by talking about the children, a topic that always relaxed her. "I hope you don't mind but I gave Josh, Wendy, and Max a sort of pre-dinner. They were so hungry that I just couldn't make them wait."

Greg's eyes swept over her, taking in her yellow blouse and knit sweater vest, the neat gray pleated skirt and low-heeled gray pumps. It was a modest, conservative school-secretary type of outfit, yet the sight of her in it aroused him more than the sight of

Francine or Linda or Debbie in their skimpiest lingerie. Lord, it was so good to see her! he thought. He'd found himself thinking about her on and off all day, in those moments when his full concentration upon his patients wasn't required.

They had parted on a sour note the day before, he'd grimly conceded to himself over the hospital cafeteria's leaden cinnamon donuts. He had behaved like a jealous fool, grabbing her like some possessive Neanderthal claiming his mate. He was determined not to repeat his mistake and scare her off. There would be no more snatching her into his arms, no matter how much he might want to. He would let her set the pace, make the first move. He *must* regain the ground he had lost with his uncharacteristic display of male dominance.

It unnerved him, that surge of possessive jealousy that had swept through him at the thought of Maggie with another man. He'd never experienced anything like it. During their long courtship and marriage, Alicia had never given him cause to feel jealous. He had been as sure of her as she'd been of him. Their relationship had been so amiable and comfortable; neither had made many demands on the other. Their lives had meshed nicely, with him being absorbed in his medical education and career and Alicia involved first in her career as a high school teacher and later with their children.

Greg frowned. He and Alicia had never quarreled or made love with the impassioned intensity that characterized his brief and volatile relationship with Maggie. He felt confused and wary, unsure if he wanted to be so totally consumed by a woman. By a woman who was holding the screen door ajar as he stood on the damn doorstep. Sudden fury pulsed through him as his desire for Maggie grew stronger. He had promised himself that he wouldn't physically overwhelm her, that he would let her set the pace and resolve their quarrel. But dammit, she wouldn't relegate him back to the doorstep while she played supermommy and clutched the door. She couldn't, not after . . .

Greg was glaring at her! Maggie thought. She took a slight step backward, still clutching the door. She'd thought—expected, hoped—that he would sweep her into his arms the moment he saw her, that their quarrel over her date would be resolved with her hugging him and telling him that she was going to break the date with Rich Cassidy. But how could she tell him anything—much less hug him—when he looked so cold, so hard, and utterly unapproachable? She backed up another step and the door nearly closed.

Dammit, Greg thought, she was still angry with him, and to prove it, she was going to keep him on the step! He was rocked by an explosive combination of incredulity and rage. She had retreated behind the door, had no intention of inviting him inside. He was back on the outside looking in, as if nothing at all had changed between them. It was enough to make him want to rip the door from its hinges.

But he wouldn't, he told himself sharply. He wasn't going to lose his cool and play savage again. That would make her retreat even further. He would show her that he could be as abominably civilized as she was.

"Thank you for giving the children something to eat," he said in an icy voice. "I agree, it's too late to make them wait for dinner. We'll stop for sandwiches on the way home."

Maggie stared at him, frozen by his tone. He hated her, she decided. He'd used that same forbidding voice when he had described the way he'd unloaded Francine. "I'll call the children," she said flatly, letting the door close. There was nothing else she could say. Greg had obviously decided that their relationship wasn't worth pursuing. Thank heavens she had resisted her impulse to throw herself into his arms when she'd answered the door. How mortifying it would have been when he had extricated himself from her embrace and told her it was over. Thank the Lord she'd been spared that!

She felt like crying as she called Wendy, Josh, and Max. The Wilder children grabbed their jackets and book bags, calling good-bye as they scampered out the door.

"How much do I owe you?" Greg asked briskly.

"Three and a half hours at three dollars an hour." Maggie computed the figures and hoped she sounded as impersonal as he. She and Greg never discussed fees. He always just handed her some money which more than covered the baby-sitting charges and included a generous tip as well. "Ten-fifty," she told him.

He handed her a ten and a five. "Keep the change," he said, and Maggie would have loved to refuse, to throw the extra bill back in his face. But that wouldn't be businesslike and Greg was making it painfully clear that it was strictly business between them.

"Can you keep Josh, Wendy, and Max on Wednesday and Friday after school until about six-thirty?" he asked coolly. "Paula has cheerleading practice on those days. Wendy and Josh will go home on the bus on Tuesday and Thursday, but Max will have to stay at the Center those days."

"I—I could bring him here," Maggie offered. She wished he would leave. It hurt to have him standing there on the doorstep, speaking so formally. She fought back one last foolish, impetuous impulse to invite him inside. Not after the man had gone out of his way to let her know that his brief desire for her had burned itself out, she thought, admonishing herself for her pitiful lack of pride.

"No, Wednesday and Friday will be enough," Greg replied. Well, he thought, he couldn't drag out his stay any longer. She'd had ample opportunity to invite him in or to make some small gesture to indicate that all was forgiven. Obviously, it wasn't. He'd scared her to death or so infuriated her that she intended to keep him safely on the doorstep, come what may. "Good night, Maggie."

"Good night, Greg." She crumpled the bills in her hand and watched Greg walk to his car where his children awaited him. The emotional letdown was terrible and she felt positively drained. All day she had been keyed up by her thoughts of Greg. For the past hour she had been breathlessly awaiting his arrival. And he had merely stood on her doorstep glaring at her.

It was even worse on Wednesday. Greg thrust the ten dollar bill at her, scowled, then turned and headed back to the car to wait for the children.

He was getting his message across, Maggie sadly acknowledged to herself. She was to forget the past weekend; she meant nothing to him. He didn't even want to resume their friendly little doorstep pleasantries.

By Friday she never wanted to hear the name Greg Wilder again. She felt used and angry and more hurt than she cared to admit. And she was most definitely going to the concert with Rich Cassidy on Saturday night.

Friday was chilly and rainy, a gloomy fall day. The weather was right in keeping with Maggie's mood. It didn't seem to matter how often she told herself that it was ridiculous to be depressed over Greg's behavior, she was still depressed. He had given her just a taste of what was missing from her life, let her glimpse what a relationship with him might bring, and then he had abruptly withdrawn himself. He'd brushed her off like an irksome mosquito. She hurt; it was useless to deny it.

The children were playing inside at five-thirty when the doorbell rang. Max, excluded from Josh and Kevin's Masters of the Universe game and uninterested in Kari and Wendy's Barbie dolls, bounded to the door to answer the bell. Maggie was close on his heels, expecting to see one or more of the Jennifers.

A strikingly pretty woman in her early twenties, wearing tight jeans and a bright orange slicker, stood on the doorstep. Definitely not a preteen Jennifer. She gave Max and Maggie a dazzling smile. "Hello." The young woman pushed her way inside and shook off the hood of her slicker. Layers of thick dark hair tumbled attractively around her shoulders. "I'm Sandy Strayer. I've come to pick up the Wilder children."

Maggie stared at her blankly. "What?"

"Greg—Dr. Wilder is running late. He asked if I would pick up the children at the baby-sitter's house and take them home. We have a date tonight at seven and he thought it would save time if I waited for him at his house and the kids were . . ." Sandy Strayer's smile faded slightly and she appeared to lose some of her zesty confidence at Maggie's expression of utter incredulity. "I'm at the right house, aren't I? Nine-oh-nine Woodland Courts? The Wilder children are supposed to be there, uh, here with their baby-sitter."

"This is nine-oh-nine and the Wilder children are here," Maggie said slowly. "I'm the baby-sitter." She saw the woman look directly at Max without a flicker of recognition. It was obvious that Sandy Strayer didn't know him, nor he her. "But I can't let the children go with you, Miss Strayer. Their father told me that he would be here at six-thirty for them, and unless I hear otherwise—"

"You just did," Sandy Strayer interrupted with a touch of asperity. "Greg asked me to pick up the kids and bring them to his house."

Maggie heaved a troubled sigh. "I'm sorry, Miss Strayer, but I'm not going to let you take the children. This is the first time I've heard of these new—um—arrangements, and since I don't know you and you don't know the kids . . ." She laid her hand on Max's shoulder. "Max, have you ever met Miss Strayer?" Max shook his head. "And since they don't know you either, I'm going to keep them here until I hear from their father."

"Look, I can understand your caution." Sandy gave Maggie a patronizing smile. "But do I look like a deranged kidnapper? I mean, really! Why would I want to take the kids home unless their father asked me to do it?"

"I'm sorry, Miss Strayer." Maggie's voice held an unmistakable note of finality. "The children are staying here."

"This is absurd! I'm a nurse at Johns Hopkins, I work on the neurosurgical floor, and I've known Dr. Wilder for nearly a whole year!" Sandy fumbled in her purse and pulled out a wallet. "Do you want proof of my identity? Here!" She thrust a collection of cards in Maggie's face. A driver's license, a registered nurse license, a hospital ID card, a Mastercard.

"You're Sandy Strayer all right," Maggie conceded. She wanted to tell the woman that it was hopeless to argue with her anymore, that her entire family—even Johnny—had always called her mule-headed and stubborn for refusing to be swayed from the course of action she'd chosen. "But the kids stay here."

"Oh!" Sandy shoved her wallet back into her handbag. "Greg forgot to warn me that I'd be dealing with a paranoic. Be reasonable, Mrs.—Ms.—" She paused, waiting for Maggie to supply her name.

"May," Maggie said obligingly. She sent Max upstairs to listen to records with Kristin. "You're welcome to wait here for Dr. Wilder, Miss Strayer," she said. "Feel free to turn on the television. Would you care for a cup of coffee or tea?"

"Aren't you afraid to be harboring a potential kidnapper?" Sandy snapped. "May I at least use your telephone, Mrs. May? If I call Greg and he confirms my story, will you let me take the kids?"

"Of course."

Greg could not be reached; he was in surgery. Sandy hung up with an angry scowl. Dinnertime came and went. Maggie fed all six children spaghetti and meatballs at the kitchen table. Sandy declined an offer of food and sat sulking in front of the television set. Maggie ate with the kids and Kristin helped her with the dishes afterward.

At seven-fifteen, the telephone rang. It was Paula Wilder. She identified herself in that startlingly adult manner of hers and then went on to ask, "Mrs. May, are my brothers and sister still at your house?"

"Yes, they are, Paula," replied Maggie.

"My father just got home and he said that they should be here. He said that he sent some woman to pick them up and bring them home."

Maggie frowned. If Greg thought he was going to conduct an argument with her using Paula as an intermediary, he was in for a surprise. "Put your father on the phone, Paula."

"Yes?" Greg's voice, cool and . . . challenging?

"Miss Strayer is here and so are your children, Dr. Wilder. Since you didn't inform me of the change in plans, I felt that I couldn't, in all good conscience, permit the children to leave with a stranger." Maggie gasped. She'd rattled off her entire mentally rehearsed speech without once pausing for breath.

"Very commendable, Mrs. May." There was no mistaking the sarcasm in his voice. "You are, as always, most conscientious."

Maggie stared at the telephone receiver in confusion. Greg seemed to be baiting her, deliberately trying to provoke her. She quickly discarded the notion. Why would he want to do that? He'd made it quite clear this past week that he wanted nothing at all to do with her.

"Has Sandy been at your house all this time," he asked, "waiting for the official word that you deem necessary to release the kids? That must have made for a rather interesting few hours."

Maggie seethed at the mockery in his voice but was determined to stay cool. "It hasn't been pleasant for either Miss Strayer or myself, Dr. Wilder. Next time I suggest that you inform me of any change in our previously made arrangements yourself."

"Shall I send you a printed itinerary of my activities? Or would you prefer to be informed of my whereabouts by telephone daily?"

He *was* trying to pick a quarrel with her. Maggie was certain of that now. But why? Their relationship had been impeccably courteous in the past, but since last weekend he had been brusque to the point of rudeness. She was tired of speculating about his motives and tired of the verbal fencing as well. "Greg, if you don't want me to baby-sit for your children anymore, just tell me so. You're not going to goad me into saying it myself. I'll tell Miss Strayer that she can leave with the children now." Maggie hung up quickly and relayed the message to Sandy, whose scowl never faded.

"We don't want to go home," complained Josh. "Can't we stay here tonight, Maggie?"

She glanced at him in surprise. Josh always called her by the more formal Mrs. May.

"It's boring at home," Wendy piped up. "Paula talks on the phone all night and Max cries and there's nothing to do."

Maggie stared at the little girl, amazed. It was the most she had ever heard Wendy say at one time in the two years she'd known her.

Maggie's thoughts turned to Max, who was in Kristin's room listening raptly to the *Top 40*, and she wondered if he would pull a number like last week's tantrum. At this rate, he probably would. It had been that kind of a day, that kind of a week.

"I'm leaving," Sandy Strayer said. She had obviously reached the end of her patience. "With or without the kids, I don't care. I've already wasted two hours here."

"The kids can stay here if they want," Maggie said, and Wendy and Josh let out a whooping cheer. Sandy stormed from the duplex in a definite huff. Maybe *she* would give Greg the fight he seemed to be seeking, Maggie thought grimly, and assured herself that she couldn't care less.

By eleven o'clock that night, all the children were tucked into bed. The whispers and the giggles and the running between rooms had gradually decreased, then ceased altogether. They were asleep at last. Maggie blessed the wonderful silence.

She changed into a pink and white candy-striped nightshirt—a Mother's Day gift from her brood—slipped on her comfortable white chenille robe and pink fuzzy slippers, and settled down with the morning paper. Who cared if the news was almost a day old? It was the only time of day that she had the time and peace to read.

When the doorbell rang a few minutes later she frowned in irritation. Who on earth could be at her door at this time of night? She thought suddenly of Mrs. Jenkins next door and her annoyance instantly turned to concern. The elderly widow was in good health, but she lived alone and Maggie made it a point to talk with her daily. But today she hadn't! It had been so hectic with all the children all evening that she'd totally forgotten her neighbor. Maggie hurried to the door, half expecting to see the police and the paramedics waiting to give her the bad news.

She opened the door, her heart thudding. Greg stood before her. She was so stunned to see him that she simply stood and stared without uttering a sound.

"I'm getting wet," Greg said at last, and Maggie finally noticed the teeming rain. The wind was blowing, rendering the small overhang useless. She was stupefied by the sight of Greg. He was truly the last person she would have expected to find on her doorstep.

"The children are in bed, asleep," she said, for she could divine no other reason for his being there.

"Thank heavens for that!" Greg muttered. He paused. And then, "May I come in or are you going to make me stand out in the rain to apologize?"

"Apologize?" Maggie echoed. She gave her head a slight shake as if to clear it. Was she dreaming?

"Yes, apologize." He'd told himself he was going to wait until she asked him in, Greg reminded himself. He'd promised himself that he wouldn't make a move until she did, that she would have to be the one to break the impasse. But it was cold standing out in the wind and rain—and he had been waiting all week for her to make that first move. And while he'd been waiting, the wall between them had grown as solid as that damned doorstep. Now it appeared that she was willing to see him soaked sooner than invite him inside. He was justified in breaking his promise to himself, he decided as he stepped inside the duplex. Maggie was forced to step aside to admit him.

He removed his wet beige raincoat, revealing a well-tailored gray suit. Maggie remembered his date that evening with Sandy Strayer and stiffened.

"Tonight was an unqualified disaster," Greg informed her, watching her intently. "Typical of most of my dates these days."

"Tomorrow is another day," Maggie quoted with acid sweetness. "Maybe you'll recoup your losses then."

"With Sandy? I don't think so. I don't think she'd go out with me again unless she was paid to do it. And it would have to be a rather hefty sum at that. She was positively furious by the time she arrived at my house. And I was in a foul mood after you and I had exchanged poisoned barbs over the phone. I made no attempt to smooth her ruffled feathers and she—"

"I'm really not interested in hearing an account of your date with Sandy Strayer," Maggie cut in coolly.

"But you would be interested in hearing my apology," he said dryly.

She looked straight ahead through the old screen door at the rain pelting the doorstep, at the porch light flickering above the mailbox. Anywhere but at Greg himself.

He took a deep breath. "It's rather difficult to

apologize to someone with the emotional range of the sphinx, but I'll give it a try. It was a rotten trick to send Sandy to pick up the kids. She sensed a setup and she was right. It was unfair to her and to the kids and"—he cleared his throat—"it was unfair to you, Maggie. I'm sorry," he added stiffly.

He didn't sound particularly sorry to Maggie. He seemed more irritated that remorseful, and prefacing his apology with that crack about the sphinx was hardly a penitent act. "Your apology, such as it is, is accepted," she said coldly. "And the next time there's a change in plans involving the children, I suggest you advise me of it yourself. And no, a printed itinerary of your schedule is not necessary."

Greg stared at her for a full ten seconds before he exploded. "Dammit, Maggie, what does it take to get through to you?"

She was startled by the sudden outburst. Greg was angry. Incredibly, furiously angry.

"Sending Sandy Strayer over here was akin to bringing in the heavy guns, but you remained as aloof as ever," he said, his eyes darkening with rage. "All week I've waited for some kind of human response from you, something, anything at all, but you've been so damned distant and utterly unreachable—"

"You're the one who's been unreachable!" cried Maggie, stung by his accusation. "You—you've barely spoken to me all week."

"How could I? You've been as inaccessible as the Army guard who patrols the Tomb of the Unknown Soldier. Have you ever tried to converse with *him*?"

"You're the one who stood on my doorstep and glared at me all week. You made that guard seem positively friendly in comparison with you, Greg Wilder."

"Where else could I stand, Mary Magdalene? I didn't rate an invitation to come inside your home. I still don't. I had to ask if I could come in, and if it hadn't been raining, you probably would have said no." He sighed with exasperation. "You really don't give a damn about me, do you, Maggie? I could spend the next ten years standing on your doorstep waiting for my kids and it wouldn't bother you at all. I'd thought that after last weekend you—that you and I . . ." He made an exclamation of disgust. "Obviously, I was wrong. My mistake."

Maggie listened with slowly dawning comprehension. "Are you saying that on Monday you expected me to ask you inside?" She'd wanted to, she remembered. She almost had. But she had been afraid to make the first move, had thought it should come from Greg. Apparently he'd had it totally reversed. While she'd been too nervous to ask him in, he had been waiting for her to do so!

"Of course I expected you to ask me in," he said. "At least I hoped you would. Having given a very convincing portrayal of a jealous idiot the day before, I could hardly compound my mistake and charge inside your house uninvited, could I?" His smile was bitter. "I hoped that you'd forgiven me for my caveman tactics, but you made it clear that you want nothing to do with me, that a cold, impersonal business relationship between us suits you just fine." He shifted his raincoat from one arm to the other. "Hell, I don't even know what I'm doing here tonight."

Her mind whirling, Maggie tried to sort out the monumental misunderstanding. Greg seemed to think their week-long estrangement was her fault! "But you've been so distant and cold all week that I assumed *you* wanted nothing to do with *me*. I thought *you'd* made it clear that you wanted a cold, impersonal business relationship."

"How could you make such an insane assumption after last weekend? You know how much I—" He swallowed, remembering their passionate urgency. Maggie remembered, too, and their eyes met and held, the shared memories alive between them. "I want you," Greg said, his voice deepening. "And you want me, too, Maggie. Don't try to deny it. The way you responded to me proved it."

"I—I wasn't going to deny it. And when you

kissed me on Sunday after we'd quarrelled . . ." Her face flushed but she kept her gaze level with his. "I didn't think you were acting like a caveman or a jealous fool, Greg," she added softly. "I wanted to see you the next day. But I didn't know you were expecting me to—to . . ."

"Make the first move?" he said.

She nodded. "When you didn't, I assumed you were letting me know you didn't want me anymore."

"Maggie, possessive and passionate exhibitions aren't exactly my style." He dropped his raincoat onto a chair. "I was more than a little disconcerted by that scene on Sunday and I promised myself that I wouldn't overwhelm you again, that I'd let you set the pace. I felt I couldn't rush inside and grab you."

"Funny thing about that," whispered Maggie. "I was expecting you to do just that." What a strange situation they'd found themselves in. Similar to stepping into a role in a play without knowing the script or the dialogue or the characters.

"So we've been at cross-purposes all week?" Greg groaned. His jewel-colored eyes were troubled. "And if I hadn't come here tonight and demanded to be let in, you would have kept withdrawing from me."

She nodded. She never would have realized that Greg was expecting any response but the one—or lack of one—that she'd given. "Did your fights with Alicia go this way?" she dared to ask. "With you waiting in silence until she made the first move to hash things out?"

"Alicia and I never fought!" he said grandly.

Maggie had to laugh at that. "Oh, come on, Greg, I was married, too, you know. All married couples fight, some more than others, of course. But even the most compatible, devoted couple has an occasional spat—unless they're a pair of real vegetables."

"So you've switched from child psychology to marriage counseling, Dr. May?" But Greg was smiling as he teased her. He shrugged. "I suppose Alicia and I did have an occasional spat or two."

"When Johnny and I fought, I was the one who withdrew until he made the first move to clear the air," Maggie said, frowning thoughtfully.

"Hmm, I see your point. Our usual withdrawal-into-silence pattern worked with Alicia and Johnny, but is disastrous for the two of us. We're going to have to work twice as hard to communicate."

Us. We. Maggie grasped at the words as harbingers of hope. That she and Greg actually were an "us" and a "we." But she didn't dare search for hidden meanings in his remarks. This past week was a perfect example of how easily she could misinterpret him.

"Now what's going on in that ever-complicated mind of yours?" he asked. "I can almost hear the wheels spinning."

"Wheels? In my head? And you're a renowned neurosurgeon?"

"Oh, no, lady, you're not going to keep me at a distance with your little jokes. I made it past the doorstep and I'll make it past your attempts at humor. We have a lot to talk about, Maggie."

He was looking at her in that certain way and Maggie felt a thrill of anticipation shoot through her. But she wasn't going to give in too easily. Not after what he'd put her through this past week. "What do you want to discuss, Dr. Wilder? The children? Baby-sitting fees?"

"Neither of the aforementioned topics, Mary Magdalene." He smiled lazily. "In fact, I don't want to talk at all. You and I have a much more direct way of communicating." He reached for her. "Don't we, Maggie?"

Six

"Do we?" Maggie whispered huskily.

Greg's hands curved slowly around her shoulders and slid up and down her arms. "I missed you this week, Maggie." His fingers moved purposefully to the belt of her robe and he carefully untied it. "I didn't realize how much I had always looked forward to your smile at the end of the day until this week when you weren't smiling for me. I even missed your stupid little jokes."

She played with his tie and the buttons on his shirt. "My jokes are not stupid. You always laughed at them, remember?"

"I remember." He slipped the robe from her shoulders and it fell in a heap at her feet. Maggie's pulses leaped. The sexual tension stretched between them, tightening to almost intolerable levels, but neither of them spoke or moved.

At last Greg's hands shifted to her waist and he slowly drew her toward him, his eyes devouring the soft curve of her lips, the firm fullness of her breasts and their taut, hard peaks. Maggie watched him watch her, mesmerized by the passion glowing in his eyes.

"I want to touch you, Maggie," he said huskily. "I've dreamed of it all week." His eyes were as caressing as his tone. "I want to feel the softness of your breasts in my hands. I want to taste your skin and kiss your nipples until you cry out for me to—"

"Greg!" She drew a deep, shuddering breath.

"Yes, like that. I want to hear you cry out my name and moan for me to take you." One hand moved up to possess her breast and a breathless little moan escaped her lips.

"Oh, Greg."

"My sweet Maggie." His voice was deep and sensual, as seductive as his lips and hands.

Maggie spun in a sensuous daze, overwhelmed by the need surging through her. She desperately wanted to feel his lips, hot and hard, upon hers, to have his tongue take possession of her mouth. She wanted to feel the hard muscles of his body against her, complementing her softness. She was an aching, burning void, wanting Greg, needing him with an intensity that both frightened and exhilarated her. Helplessly, hungrily, she watched his mouth lazily descend toward hers. When she felt the touch of his lips, her eyelids closed heavily and she opened her mouth to him.

She sighed deeply as his tongue probed the sweet warmth within. How had she managed to survive this week—this lifetime—without his kisses? she wondered dizzily. She leaned into him, allowing his strong frame to absorb her weight. It was sheer heaven to be held by him this way. She felt so safe, so secure, yet so excited in his arms.

His hands were all over her, smoothing the soft cotton of her nightshirt against her skin, caressing every curve as he pressed her closer to him. She permitted her own hands to wander over the rippling muscles of his back, but was frustrated by the clothing separating her from his bare skin. A T-shirt, a blue oxford cloth shirt, his vest and suit coat—four layers!

"You have too many clothes on," she murmured, her voice husky with an alluring combination of passion and humor. Standing on tiptoe, she nibbled at his earlobe while his lips investigated the tender hollow at the base of her throat.

"Would you like to undress me?" he asked as he trailed a path of little stinging kisses along the curve of her neck.

"Would you like me to?" Her tongue daringly teased the inner shell of his ear and he groaned and lifted her slightly, positioning her firmly between the solid columns of his thighs. Maggie felt the burgeoning force of his need and clung to him. "Oh, Lord, yes, Maggie. Yes, please darling."

It was an urgent, heartfelt plea. Maggie gazed into his striking eyes and emotion surged through her, a warm union of tenderness and passion that felt strangely akin to . . . love?

"Let me stay with you tonight, Maggie," he said, holding her tightly as if he feared she might suddenly break away.

The mother in Maggie surfaced. "Your children are here tonight, too, Greg. What will we tell them, and mine, if—"

"We'll lock the bedroom door. We'll say I came over to pick the kids up and you offered to show me your photo albums or something. I don't know. At this point I don't care. We'll think of something."

"But what if—" She broke off abruptly as he leaned down and swept her up in his arms. He lifted her as easily as he might one of the little children. "You're so strong," she gasped breathlessly, and then blushed. She sounded like the vacuous heroine of an even more vacuous teen movie. With her self-criticism came doubt. Did she really want to go through with this? Her stomach churned with nervous uncertainty. Everything had happened so fast. She hadn't had time to think things through. "Greg," she began hesitantly.

"You'll have to direct me to your room." He was already carrying her up the stairs, and he smiled into her eyes. "Left to my own devices, I'd probably stumble into the kids' rooms and wake them all up. Do you think they'd believe you twisted your ankle and asked me to help you up the stairs?"

She managed to smile. "They'd believe it sooner than the photo album story. I keep the albums downstairs and all the kids know it."

Greg had reached the top of the stairs. "Left or right?" he whispered, brushing his lips against her temple.

She turned her face into his shoulder. "Greg, I know this is going to sound foolish—I mean, I am thirty-two years old and the mother of three children—but I'm"—she swallowed—"I'm as nervous right now as I was on my wedding night." There, she had said it. She waited apprehensively for his reply, expecting either a flippant joke or a well-oiled statement designed to soothe her nerves and allow him to proceed.

"I know, honey," he said. "I feel a little nervous too."

She blinked in confusion. Whatever she'd been expecting him to say, it hadn't been that!

"You're . . . special, Maggie," Greg said slowly, as if groping for the words. "And I want it to be so good for you, for us. I'm not saying this because I think it's what you want to hear. I want you very badly, you know that, but if you have any doubts, sweetheart, I—I can wait until you're absolutely certain."

The tension and the nervous uncertainty were dissolved by the sincerity in his voice. Greg Wilder was only a few steps from her bedroom and her imminent surrender, yet he had the strength of character to stop if she wished. Just knowing that erased her doubts. She cared for Greg Wilder; she wanted him. He was thoughtful and generous, a caring father, a dedicated doctor. She admired him and respected him. There had been only one other man in her life with whom she'd felt this sense of rightness, and that had been her husband. But not even with Johnny had she experienced this passionate hunger, this burning drive to be one with him. "I'm sure now, Greg," she whispered. "My room is on the left."

Greg carried her into her bedroom and laid her gently down on the bed. He lay down beside her and they kissed, lightly at first, then with increasing demand. "When are you going to get me out of these clothes?" he teased as she clung to him.

"I'm trying, I'm trying." Maggie laughed as she fumbled with the buttons on his vest. "I haven't had a whole lot of experience with custom-tailored suits." She was no longer embarrassed, but felt relaxed and at ease with Greg. There was no awkwardness between them now. It was as if they had lain in bed together many times before.

"Maybe I'd better take off my suit and hang it up," he suggested. "Unless you wouldn't mind doing a quick steam and press in the morning?"

"I'd mind." She gave him a playful push. "Hang up your clothes and hurry back to me."

He did, carefully locking the door before he returned to the bed. "That should discourage any nighttime visitors," he said with a wolfish grin. "And now, my sweet . . ."

Maggie quickly reached up to turn off the bedside lamp. "No." Greg stayed her hand. "Leave it on, Maggie. I don't want to grope and fumble in the dark. I want to be able to see you, to watch you."

She felt a flush of hot color slowly suffuse her body. No one had ever watched her. "Greg, I'd feel, er, more comfortable if—"

"I'll make sure you're perfectly comfortable, sweetheart," he interrupted, a devilish gleam in his eyes. "Come here." He pulled her into his arms and sighed. "Maggie, I don't know what I would have done if you had sent me away tonight."

"I—I couldn't have, Greg," she confessed. Her hands glided over the satisfying smoothness of his bare back and slid round to tangle in the wiry mat of dark blond hair on his chest. She touched a hard nipple, then caressed it lightly with her thumb. "I like to touch you," she said shyly, feeling the need to explain herself.

He caught her hand and kissed the palm, then each finger in turn. "I like to have you touch me." His hands slid under the hem of her nightshirt and lifted it slowly, carefully, over her head. He tossed it casually to the floor. "And I love to touch you, darling, to look at you." His eyes swept her body and Maggie caught her breath.

She knew what her body looked like and it wasn't like the Playmate of any month. She had stretch marks on her abdomen, courtesy of three pregnancies. Her stomach muscles were too soft, her belly slightly rounded. If only she'd stuck to that killer regimen of sit-ups. Alas, she hadn't. What was Greg thinking? she wondered. Was he comparing her to other women he had known, young goddesses with firm, beautiful bodies? She trembled slightly, asking herself why she had ever let herself in for this intimate appraisal.

"I told you it would be better with the lights out," she said, making a brave attempt at humor. "Then you could pretend I was lithe and firm and twenty-two."

"Is that what you think I want?" He held her eyes with his.

"What man wouldn't?" she retorted flippantly.

"Me, for one."

"Oh, I see. You prefer women over thirty with stretch marks and flabby muscles to gorgeous young creatures like Francine and Sandy Strayer. Now why am I having a hard time believing that?"

Greg astonished her by grinning. "Oh, no, Mary Magdalene. I see what you're trying to do and it isn't going to work. You're feeling scared and hoping to start a fight that will send me away—or permit *you* to send me away."

"That's not true!"

"Isn't it?" He ran his fingertips lightly over the tops of her thighs. "Isn't it, Maggie?"

She swallowed, her green eyes clouding. "I don't think it's true." His fingers darted teasingly to the apex of her thighs and she quivered.

"Now why am I having a hard time believing that?" he drawled mockingly. He chuckled softly, dangerously, and grazed her parted lips with his mouth. "What do you really want, Maggie?" His long fingers took possession of one taut, aching nipple. "Tell me, honey."

A soft, high-pitched moan escaped her throat as he continued to tease her with that maddening finger. "I think I already know." His hand closed over her breast as he tantalized her mouth with his. "You want me to love you, don't you, sweetheart?"

"Yes," Maggie breathed, and she knew in that instant that she really did want him to love her, and not just physically. She wanted what the songwriters called true love, a physical and emotional and spiritual commitment to last forever. "Oh, Greg," she murmured. The realization shattered her final inhibitions and replaced her feelings of inadequacy with the powerful urge to please Greg, to give him whatever he needed to make him happy. "I want you so much."

"No more nervous little doubts?" he whispered softly.

She shook her head with a loving smile. "I want to make love, Greg."

His hard body shuddered with the words and his hands moved over her in enticing exploration. Shivering with sensation, Maggie did a little exploring of her own. "Yes, love, touch me," he said, then groaned as she found the straining force of his masculinity. "Ok, Maggie, I feel like I'm going out of my mind."

Maggie was filled with a heady sense of feminine power. It was thrilling to know that she could arouse Greg to such a state. Conversely, she wanted to relieve his need, to give him a kind of pleasure he could never find with anyone else.

His fingers tangled in the thatch of auburn curls

and she sucked in her breath as he caressed the ultrasensitive core of her passion. The flowing warmth he found there told him that her desire was as strong as his own.

"Greg," she cried out as waves of sensual rapture consumed her. "Oh, Greg, please!"

"Yes, Maggie, yes, love," he said thickly. "Are you protected, Maggie, or shall I . . .?"

She blinked in momentary confusion. "I hadn't even thought about it," she whispered, and he smiled.

"Then I'll take care of you, darling," he said softly as he eased off the bed. Moments later he came back to her and she welcomed him, their bodies merging slowly and completely.

She emitted a wild little cry and arched upward to meet the hard, urgent thrust of his body. Greg whispered something incredibly dark and sexy before he took her mouth with bold possession. Maggie felt the stirrings of a wild, savage sweetness as her body tightened with a violent intensity. It was happening, she thought dizzily. What she had read about, what she had assumed was mere media propaganda, was actually happening to her.

"Don't hold back, Maggie," Greg whispered. "Just let go, baby. Give yourself to me, come to me."

She did and he took her with him on an ecstatic, mind-shattering ascent to the summits of rapture. She had never experienced anything quite like it. And when Greg joined her in the shimmering release of their passion, she felt a wholeness, a completeness she had never known. . . .

Maggie snuggled deeper into Greg's arms, her head on his chest, her legs comfortably entwined with his. He stroked her hair lightly with his big hand. *I love him*, she thought drowsily. Her defenses completely eradicated, it was easy to admit the truth to herself. But saying the words to Greg was another matter. "You're wonderful" was the closest she dared to come, and she sighed and said it again. "You're wonderful, Greg. It was wonderful." Beneath her ear she felt Greg's chest rumble with soft laughter.

"One always likes to be praised for a good performance. Thank you, gracious lady. You were rather wonderful yourself."

Maggie considered setting the record straight, telling Greg that it wasn't his performance she was praising, that he'd misinterpreted her, that she'd really meant to say that she loved him. But she decided against it. He had set the mood as playful and light. It was not the time for heavy emotional confessions. So she reached up to tweak his nose mischievously and murmur sexily, "Only *rather* wonderful, Dr. Wilder?"

"All right, wonderfully wonderful," he corrected himself, and kissed her lingeringly. "Now go to sleep, lady. You've thoroughly exhausted me."

He didn't want to talk, Maggie thought. She was feeling an almost compulsive need to discuss what had just happened between them, how she felt, how he felt, everything and anything pertaining to themselves and what they'd shared. But Greg had switched off the light and lay silent. She swallowed her disappointment and tried to understand. Of course the poor man was tired. He'd had a grueling day at the hospital, it was past midnight. Of course he wanted to sleep. She would be content to hold him in her arms all night long, savoring his nearness and—She bolted upright in bed. "Greg, are you going to stay here all night?"

"Don't you want me to stay, Maggie?"

"Yes, but what will we tell the kids in the morning?"

"Leave the kids to me." He tugged her back down to him. "I'll think of something to tell them tomorrow. Now go to sleep, love."

She cuddled closer. "Good night, Greg." How

wonderful to go to sleep in his arms and wake up with him in the morning. She sighed.

Greg kissed her temple. "Good night, sweetheart."

"Oh, no! Greg, what about Paula?" She again sat up abruptly. "I forgot all about her. She can't stay alone all night."

"Relax, honey." Again Greg pulled her back down and settled her in his arms. "She's spending the night with one of her girlfriends. Maggie, if Paula *were* home alone, you'd have insisted that I leave, wouldn't you?" His arms tightened possessively and his tone was thoughtful. "You would have sent me home to her."

"Of course. She's only fourteen. That's too young to be left alone all night, Greg."

"Oh, *I* know that. But you're the first woman that I've—uh—" He stopped, then began again. "The first woman who has ever agreed that the kids shouldn't be alone all night. Every other one has bitched and complained when I told them that I had to go home, er, áfterward."

Every one of Maggie's nerves was seared by the jealous flame that ripped through her. Every other woman. "I'd rather not hear about all your other women," she managed to say in frozen tones. How awful it was to be catapulted from a cozy dream world into the depressing throes of reality. Tonight had been so special to her, an affirmation of her womanhood with the man she loved. To her it had marked the beginning of a loving relationship and she had given herself completely, as if the feelings had been mutual.

But they weren't, a fact she had somehow managed to forget. Tonight couldn't have been particularly special or unique for Greg. To him she was merely another woman in another bed on another Friday night. Last week it would have been Francine, had she not thrown her nasty little tantrum. Tonight it was supposed to have been Sandy, but she had also staged a scene. It was anybody's guess as to who he had lined up for next week, but if the woman managed to hang on to her temper she would undoubtedly wind up in bed with Greg.

Maggie rolled out of his arms and onto her side, dragging the covers around her.

"Maggie?" Greg reached for her, his voice filled with confusion.

"Good night, Greg."

"Come back here!"

"I'm very tired and you told me that you're tired too. I'd like to get some sleep before the kids get up at seven."

"But what . . . Maggie, are you angry with me? What in the hell is going on with you?"

"Just think about it, Greg. I'm sure a smart fellow like you will come up with some satisfactory answer."

"I was complimenting you." He seemed to be mentally reviewing their conversation. "You're the first and only woman to have expressed concern about my children spending the night alone, the first and only one who hasn't—"

"I'm sorry I don't have any interesting comparisons to share with you," Maggie said tightly, sexual jealousy eating at her like acid. "But you're the first and only man I've been with since my husband was killed six years ago. The first and only one, and so—"

"Six years!" Greg shook his head, awed. "That's an incredibly long time to be without, uh, love."

"You mean sex," she corrected him tartly, sitting up to glare at him. "And it wasn't all that difficult. When you're working the night shift and taking care of small children during the day, believe me, the need for sex takes second place to the need for sleep."

"But now you're working days and the children are in school and . . ." Greg paused, frowning. "You accepted a date with Cassidy and went to bed with me."

"Don't you dare insinuate that I'm about to become some sort of sexual adventuress!" she snapped. "I'm not, I assure you."

"Maggie, I wasn't insinuating any such thing. It simply occured to me that—"

"Not everyone has your insatiable need for—for bedroom adventures, Greg Wilder."

"Bedroom adventures? I would hardly call my—"

"Perhaps conquests would be the better word," she suggested sweetly. "Or would exploits be even better?"

Greg sat up in bed and clutched his head with his fingers. "You're doing it again, Maggie. You're driving me up the wall. You seem to have a special talent for it. Five minutes ago I was holding you, loving you, and now I'm ready to toss you out the window. If I don't jump out myself first," he added grimly.

"Why not leave the way you came? Through the door. Now!"

"Are you asking me to leave?"

"No, I'm telling you. Good-bye, Greg Wilder!" Maggie pulled the covers up to her nose and rolled onto her stomach, effectively wrapping herself in a blanket cocoon. She could hear Greg moving about in the darkness, hear the rustling of his clothes as he dressed. First the white cotton briefs and T-shirt . . . She tried desperately to banish the image of his muscular, tanned body in the formfitting underwear, but the picture was firmly fixed in her mind's eye. Taunting her, tantalizing her.

She swallowed back a sob of pure misery. She wanted to beg him to stay, but she feared his rejection, his scorn. Never had she felt so vulnerable and so terribly at risk. Hot tears burned her eyes, but she blinked them away. Crying was for tragedies, like Johnny's death. She wouldn't trivialize her tears by weeping over Greg Wilder's angry departure.

"Maggie!" The clear, childish voice filled the silent house. "Maggie, where are you?"

It was Max. Maggie threw off the covers, grabbed her robe, and quickly slipped into it. "I'm coming, Max," she called in a loud whisper. She hoped he could hear her.

"I'll go to him," Greg said. He was wearing his trousers and holding his shirt in his hands. He dropped it on the bed and followed Maggie into Kevin's bedroom. Kevin and Josh were asleep in the bunk beds. Max was sitting up in the small cot, crying.

"Max, honey, what is it?" Maggie scooped him up in her arms.

"There's a bad wolf in this room. A werewolf with great big teeth. He said he was going to eat me up." Max put his small arms around Maggie's neck and hung on tightly.

"Were Josh and Kevin telling scary stories before you went to sleep?" she asked softly.

Max nodded. "Werewolfs live in closets and under the bed and eat people up," he whimpered. "I'm scared, Maggie."

"There's nothing to be afraid of, Max." Greg moved to stand beside Maggie and he patted his son's head. "There are no such things as werewolves."

"Are too," sniffed Max. "Josh said so." He didn't even question his father's half-dressed, late-night appearance at the Mays'.

"Now who knows more, Josh or Daddy?" Greg said. He tried to take Max from Maggie's arms, but the little boy wouldn't release the grip he had on her neck. "Daddy knows more," Greg answered his own question. "And I say there is no such thing as were-wolves. Look." He flicked on a lamp and opened the closet door. "There's nothing in the closet but Kevin's clothes and some toys."

Max frowned and continued to cling to Maggie, his arms and legs wrapped around her. Greg got down on his hands and knees and made an elaborate display of looking under both bunks and the cot. "No werewolf here either. Not even any dustballs. You're an excellent housekeeper, Maggie," he added ingenuously and smiled at her. She had to smile back at him; she simply couldn't help herself.

Max, however, wasn't smiling. "It's an invisible

werewolf, Daddy. You can't see him, but he's there. Can I sleep in your bed, Maggie?" he pleaded. "A werewolf can't get me there."

"No, Max," Greg intervened quickly. "Four-year-olds are too big to sleep in other people's beds."

Max looked ready to cry again. Maggie gave him a quick hug and suddenly an idea dawned. She'd once had this same problem with Kari and the solution she'd come up with then had worked like a charm. Perhaps she would have equal luck with Max.

"Look at this, Max." Maggie picked up one of Kevin's creations, a gun made out of Tinkertoy pieces. "Do you know what this is?"

Max shook his head.

"It's a magic zapper. You draw a cricle around your bed"—Maggie drew a wide imaginary circle around Max's cot with the stick-gun—"and it produces a ring of invisible energy. Nothing can get through the invisible magic ring unless you invite it in. Here." She handed the gun to Max. "You try it."

Max drew a somewhat haphazard imaginary circle. "Your bed is doubly protected now," Maggie said. "Any werewolf who comes near the magic circle will be bounced off it."

"Will it burn him?" Max asked hopefully.

"Oh, yes. And if you want to give him an extra zap, just point the magic zapper at him." She stretched out her hand and moved it around. "I think I can feel the energy, Max."

Max clutched the zapper, his eyes wide. "Me too," he breathed.

Maggie set him down in the cot. "You hold onto the zapper, Max. It's yours to keep." She tucked him under the covers and kissed his cheek. "Good night, Max. You have nothing to worry about now."

Max gave her an extra squeeze. " 'Night, Maggie." He held out his free arm to his father. "Hug, Daddy." Greg bent down and Max wrapped one small arm around his father's neck, keeping his other around

Maggie's. Their faces were very close as each kissed the little boy's cheek.

Greg and Maggie left the room together, and when Greg glanced over his shoulder, he saw Max waving the zapper around in the air. "He bought the whole story," he whispered admiringly as they stood in the hall. "He's never settled down so easily after a nightmare. How did you ever come up with that zapper idea, Maggie?"

She shrugged. "I've learned from my own kids that simply telling them that something scary doesn't exist won't work. Small children sometimes have a hard time distinguishing fantasy from reality. And anyone who believes that an invisible werewolf is in the closet will have no trouble believing in a magic zapper that will create a protective barrier."

Greg broke into a broad grin. "It's so simple. Why didn't I think of it years ago? We've been through night lights, searches for monsters in the middle of the night . . ." He shook his head, bemused, then put an arm around Maggie's shoulder and drew her to his side. "Did you notice that Max didn't even question why I was here in the middle of the night wearing only my trousers?"

"When you're four years old and battling werewolves, a late-night appearance by your father must not seem like anything out of the ordinary," Maggie said dryly. Then she started to step away from him, but he tightened his hold on her.

"Are we still fighting, Maggie?" He cupped her chin in his hand and tilted her head upward. "Whatever I did to upset you, I apologize."

"That covers all bases." She couldn't find the words to tell him how his casual attitude toward their lovemaking had wounded her, making her sensitive to his every remark. "But I suppose I did overreact," she added. She wanted words from him which he could not or would not say. It wasn't fair to be angry with him because he didn't love her.

His eyes were holding hers. "Maggie, I don't want to leave you tonight. May I stay?"

She wanted him to stay with all her heart. Their earlier argument seemed stupid and irrelevent. He didn't love her, but she loved him and wanted him with her. "Yes, Greg," she murmured. "Please stay." This time she would expect nothing, would make no unspoken demands. They walked into the bedroom, their arms around each other.

"Maggie," came Max's voice.

"What is it, Max?" She suppressed a smile at Greg's expression of chagrin.

"It works, Maggie. The zapper works. The werewolf is too scared to come out."

"That's good, Max," she called in an equally loud whisper. "You go to sleep now."

"The magic zapper works," Greg said, pulling her into his arms. "Will you give me some of your magic too, Maggie?" His fingers quickly dispensed with the tie of her robe. And then with the robe itself.

"Now? Again?" she said. A melting warmth swept through her.

"Yes, now." He nibbled on her lips, his tongue teasing hers. "Yes, again."

"I thought you were tired. You wanted to go right to sleep," she reminded him, moving sinuously against his hard frame.

"Well, I'm awake now." His hands cupped her buttocks. "And I never felt less like sleeping in my life." He thrust against her with urgent male proof of his claim. "Please, honey."

"Well . . . since you're begging," she said lightly. "I'll think about it." She would make herself appear as casual about it as he. And when he withdrew after making love to her, she wouldn't be disappointed, she promised herself.

"You'll think about it? You like to live dangerously, don't you, little tease?" Greg growled and slowly lowered her onto the bed. They kissed deeply, passionately. "I want you so much, Maggie," he said hoarsely. "Sweetheart, I have to have you."

She wrapped her arms around him with a soft sigh and surrendered to the combined forces of passion and love flowing within her. This time their lovemaking was leisurely and tender, as if having satisfied their first volatile and passionate needs, they could now afford to take the time to be gentle. But the end results were the same for Maggie—an intense, explosive climax that left her replete and glowing and clinging to Greg, wildly in love. Bonded to him, body and heart and soul.

"Maggie?" His voice was quiet and low in the now darkened room.

She was already drifting into sleep, snuggled deep in his arms. "Hmm?" She didn't open her eyes. She could never remember feeling so deliciously relaxed.

"Break your date with Cassidy tomorrow."

Her eyes snapped open and she tensed, turning her head to look at him. They were so close that she could easily discern the stubborn set of his jaw and his blazing jeweled eyes. "Oh, Greg!" She sighed wearily. "Did you have to bring that up now?"

"Break the date, Maggie. You know you don't want to go out with him."

"True," she admitted with a yawn. "But I told him I would go to the concert with him and it doesn't seem right to back out at the last minute."

"Never break one date for another. I bet your mother told you that back in high school. I've given a similar spiel to Paula. That's one of the Official Rules of Teen Dating. It's considered character building for adolescents to suffer through dates with the wrong person simply because they said yes at a weak moment." Greg traced the shape of her mouth with one long finger. "But those rules don't apply in our case, Maggie. We're long past adolescence. We don't need stupid guidelines. We set our own."

"Greg, I realize that I last dated back in the Dark

Ages, but it still seems rude to break a date just because"—she paused and stroked the rough skin of his cheek with her fingertips—"someone more interesting comes along."

"Well, I'm glad you at least concede that I'm more interesting than Cassidy." Greg caught her hand and carried it to his mouth, tickling her palm with his tongue. Maggie quivered. "Break the date, Maggie. I want to be with you tomorrow night."

Oh, she wanted it too. But mother-ingrained rules die hard. "Greg, the concert will only last a couple of hours. It'll be so much easier if I just go with him. I have to see the man every Thursday at school, he's getting Kevin a used trumpet at a great price and will be giving him music lessons, and—"

"I'll buy Kevin a brand-new trumpet and pay for private music lessons. Break the date first thing in the morning, Maggie."

Why did everything have to be so complicated? she thought. Especially when she was groggy from lack of sleep. She couldn't think clearly, couldn't think things through . . .

"I don't want to argue with you, Greg. And—and I don't want another week of frozen silence like this past one either. Please try to understand."

"Understand what? That you prefer to spend tomorrow night with the clod who kicked my little girl out of the junior high band?"

Maggie groaned. She couldn't rehash it *again!* She could hardly keep her eyes open. "I'm exhausted, Greg. I just want to go to sleep."

"And dream of Cassidy and his used trumpet?"

She kicked him with her bare foot. "I'm not going to dream of anyone but you, Greg Wilder, and you know it."

"You'll be sorry if you keep your date with Cassidy, Maggie," Greg said pleasantly. Too pleasantly. Had she been more alert, her suspicions might have been aroused. "That's both a promise and a threat, honey," he added in the same light tone.

Maggie wasn't alarmed. He wasn't angry with her, he couldn't be, she thought sleepily. He was holding her so tenderly, stroking her hair so lovingly. She cuddled closer and closed her eyes.

"Maggie?" Greg was holding her hand in his, his thumb moving over her gold wedding ring. "I want you to take this ring off."

Her heart missed a beat. She'd always worn her wedding ring, night and day, for the past thirteen years.

"I don't want to be in bed with another man's wife, Maggie. And as long as you wear that ring you're Johnny's wife, if only symbolically."

She slipped the ring off without a word. It was time. She felt no disloyalty to Johnny, none at all. But her finger did feel bare and strange without the accustomed wide band.

Greg watched her as she placed the ring in the small drawer of the nightstand. "Come here," he whispered. She turned to him. "I've never thought of myself as the possessive type, Maggie. But seeing that ring on your finger as you lay here in bed with me . . ." His voice trailed off. He wondered if he sounded as surprised and confused as he felt by these unexpected, strange feelings coursing through him. His arms tightened around Maggie in possession.

She nestled her head against his shoulder. "I won't wear it anymore, Greg," she promised.

Seven

It was a few minutes past nine when Maggie stirred and woke to find herself alone in the bed. The room was still dark, the curtains drawn, and she heard rain pounding against the windows. The lateness of the hour shocked her. She couldn't remember the last time—if ever—she'd slept as late as nine. Memories of the night before washed over her in sensual waves and she blushed hotly. She couldn't remember the last time—if ever—she'd spent a night like last night either.

She climbed slowly out of bed, her body voluptuously sore in certain places. She stumbled into the shower, still slightly dazed, not allowing herself to think. That could be dangerous. Glancing down at her ringless hand, she forced herself to concentrate on the automatic tasks of showering, shampooing her hair, and blowing it dry. She dressed quickly in jeans and a yellow turtleneck and nervously brushed her hair. She dreaded going downstairs. Was Greg there? And what could she say to all the children? What had he said? The prospect of facing her lover with six interested observers present was truly a daunting one.

It was extremely anticlimactic to find Kristin, Kevin, and Kari sitting in front of the TV set watching cartoons, just as they did every other Saturday morning. The Wilders were gone, all four of them.

"Hi, Mom." Kristin glanced away from the television as Maggie entered the room. "Are you feeling better?"

Maggie gave her a blank stare. "What?"

"Dr. Wilder said that when he called last night to tell you what time he would pick up the kids, you told him you weren't feeling well," Kristin explained. "He said that you needed to sleep and we weren't to wake you up."

Maggie again had the queer sensation of having walked into the middle of a play and being expected to follow the action without knowing the plot. "When did you talk to Dr. Wilder, Kristin?" she asked carefully.

"He came by real early this morning, before seven o'clock. None of us were awake, but he kept ringing the doorbell until I woke up and let him in. I was kind of scared when you didn't wake up, Mommy," she confessed. "Dr. Wilder said he would look in on you and make sure you were all right."

Maggie was aware that she was blushing fiercely. She visualized Greg walking into her bedroom and looking at her as she slept naked beneath the covers. But then, she'd been sleeping naked with him all night! She touched her burning cheeks with hands that were icy cold. Thankfully, Kristin's attention had been claimed by a soft drink commercial that she found far more interesting than her mother.

Maggie struggled to regain her composure. The Wilders were gone and Greg had managed to dress, leave the house, locking the door behind him, in order to pretend he was just arriving to pick up his children. Obviously none of the kids knew that he'd spent the night there and Maggie was deeply relieved that they didn't. She didn't know how to explain, what to say. She didn't even know when she would see Greg again. Her thoughts raced as madly as her pulses. Song titles to the contrary, it wasn't easy falling in love. Not at age thirty-two, when you had three children and he had four. Nor was love particularly comfortable the second time around. This was more confusing and passionate and intensely encompassing than the first time had ever been.

The cartoon show ended and Kevin looked up, acknowledging his mother's presence for the first time. "The soccer game was called off because of the rain," he said morosely. "I don't have anything to do."

"Why don't you invite Josh over to play?" Maggie suggested. She was embarrassed by her overtly obvious conniving. If Kevin called Josh, she would have to talk to Greg to make arrangements for the boys to play. She thought of Taffy Smithton, who had engineered a similar ploy, and cringed. What was she turning into?

"The Wilders are going somewhere today," Kristin said. "I heard Dr. Wilder tell the kids."

"Where are they going?" Maggie asked, far too quickly.

Kristin shrugged. "To some friend's house. Lynn something. I can't remember the last name."

Lynn. It could be either masculine or feminine, Maggie told herself. Was the Lynn with whom Greg and his children planned to spend the day—and possibly the night—a man or a woman?

It was most surely a woman, she decided with certainty, and was sickened by her jealousy and uneasiness. Why had she been so foolish as to fall in love with Greg Wilder? Her life had been so placid, so predictable, so peacefully dull before she'd committed that folly. She didn't want or need the trauma of an emotional involvement.

The rest of the morning dragged. Maggie scrubbed the bathroom and the kitchen; she changed the sheets on all the beds; she did some laundry; she dusted and vacuumed. The physical activity kept her occupied, but her thoughts were focused obsessively on Greg. "You'll be sorry if you keep your date with Cassidy," he'd said. "That's both a promise and a threat." Did he mean to punish her by spending the day (and night) with the woman named Lynn? What if he again subjected her to the silent treatment? Maggie's heart contracted with pain. She didn't think she could bear it, not after last night, not after what they'd shared. But the facts remained: She was going out with Rich Cassidy and Greg was with someone named Lynn. No doubt he had purposely dropped her name, knowing that Kristin would repeat it. He probably wanted her to be tortured by jealous suspicions all day!

The afternoon brought the Jamison children and an unexpected baby-sitting job. The three active preschoolers kept Maggie frantically busy, and Kevin, Kristin, and Kari all had friends over as well. The noise level in the house was deafening. Maggie was relieved when Mr. Jamison arrived to collect his brood at five o'clock and she sent the friends home shortly afterward.

The telephone rang just as she was sinking down onto the sofa. It was the first time she'd dared to sit since the Jamisons had arrived at one. "Will one of you kids answer the phone?" She said to her children.

"I will, Mommy!" Kari raced into the kitchen. "Mommy?" she called moments later. "Are you still going on that date tonight?"

"Yes," Maggie sighed, wishing she weren't. She felt physically as well as emotionally drained. The thought of making polite small talk with Rich Cassidy was truly debilitating.

"Mommy, where is the date?" Kari called. And then she corrected herself. "Where is the concert?"

Kari didn't know words like concert. Someone—on the phone—was asking her questions. Maggie headed instantly to the kitchen. Kari was clutching the telephone receiver. "It's Dr. Wilder, Mommy."

"Greg?" Maggie's voice was more like a breathless squeak.

"So you're still going to go through with it?"

Greg's voice was smooth as silk. "I did tell you that you're going to regret it, didn't I?"

"Did you have a nice day with Lynn?" Maggie fired back. No one told her what she could or couldn't do, least of all Greg Wilder, who had a different date every week.

"I had a wonderful time. Where is this concert you and Cassidy plan to attend?"

The question caught her off-guard. She was still smarting over his enthusiastic reply to *her* question. "At the Woodland Civic Center. It's a woodwind and percussion group."

Greg gave a low whistle. "Woodwind *and* percussion? Now there's a dream come true."

"Greg—"

"If you insist on going, Maggie, there is nothing more to be said. Just remember I warned you." His silky tones unnerved her. "Good-bye, Maggie." He hung up before she could reply.

Rich Cassidy complimented Maggie on her cream-colored dress. Maggie complimented him on his tie. They discussed the weather (still raining), the traffic (moderate for this time Saturday night), and this year's elementary school band (promising) on the brief drive to the Civic Center. Rich was not exactly loquacious, and by the time they had settled into their seats at the plush Woodland public auditorium, they seemed to have exhausted their entire supply of conversation.

She could have been with Greg, Maggie reminded herself gloomily as the musicians tuned their instruments and she and Rich sat in uncomfortable silence. Rich dropped his program for the fifth time and when she reached down to retrieve it, he stepped on her hand. She jerked up so quickly that she didn't notice that he had bent over. Their heads collided. Rich's lip bled; Maggie could feel his toothmark in the back of her head. Many mutually embarrassed apologies followed. Maggie lapsed back into gloom. Yes, she could have been with Greg, but she had stubbornly elected to follow the Official Rules of Teen Dating, at age thirty-two.

She decided it was not at all character building to suffer through a date with the wrong person. It was depressing and boring. And painful. Her hand and her head still hurt from the collision with Rich's foot and tooth. It was also unnecessary. She had removed her wedding ring when Greg had asked her to. Why hadn't she broken this date at his request as well? It was one of those questions without an answer. Greg had said she would regret this date and he was absolutely right.

The lights dimmed and the musicians placed their instruments in position. And just at that moment Greg Wilder and seven children trooped down the aisle to a group of seats five rows in front of where Maggie sat with Rich Cassidy. She gasped, wondering if she were hallucinating. She half-hoped that she was.

But it was the flesh-and-blood Greg who was carrying Max and holding Kari by the hand. Wendy and Kristin followed, then Kevin and Joshua and a pretty teenage girl who could only be Paula Wilder. Kevin was lugging a big shopping bag.

"Okay, who wants some caramels? Who wants some M & M's?" Maggie heard her son say as they settled in their seats. "Marshmallows? Bubble gum? Jelly beans?"

Maggie sat as still as a stone. Rich cleared his throat. "Er, aren't they, uh, your children down there with Dr. Wilder?" he asked uneasily. He'd just met them at the duplex twenty minutes earlier.

Maggie gradually emerged from her paralysis. Her first emotion was that of maternal horror. Her children were still wearing their old sweatshirts and jeans, the ones they'd worn all day. Kari had gotten mustard on the front of her shirt at dinner; Kevin's hair was uncombed and askew. She was certain that all three had on their oldest sneakers with holes in the toes.

"You, er, didn't mention that your kids were coming tonight," said Rich, and Maggie wanted to hit him. Did he actually think that she would allow her children to appear at a posh place like the Civic Center looking like a ragtag tribe from Poverty Row? She was fiercely proud of her children. Whenever they went anywhere she took great care to see that they were properly groomed and well-dressed. Their teachers often complimented her on their neat appearance. And Rich Cassidy thought she would send them to the Civic Center on a Saturday night dressed for yard work? "I didn't know the children were coming," she replied tightly.

Kevin was still passing out candy. There was more junk in that bag than Maggie allowed them to have for Halloween and Christmas combined. Pounds and pounds of candy. They were going to be flying on a sugar high all night—and the dental bills! Maggie shuddered. Kristin and Kari were already cavity-prone.

"Do you know Dr. Wilder well?" Rich asked, then gave a nervous little laugh. "What a stupid question! Of course you do, your children wouldn't be here with him if you didn't."

Maggie made no reply. Her eyes were fixed on the kids, who were tearing open candy wrappers, whispering too loudly, and traipsing from one seat to another. Not one of them appeared to be listening to the clarinet duo on stage. The woman sitting behind them shushed them twice and Greg turned around to give her a dark glare. Then his gaze shifted and rested lingeringly on Maggie.

It was dark and they were six rows apart, but Maggie was completely aware of the message in his mocking eyes. "You'll be sorry . . . I warned you . . ." He'd kept his promise and carried out his threat. The beast!

Rich shifted in his seat and Maggie cast a covert

glance at him. He was watching Greg and the children too. When he caught her eye he leaned over and whispered, "I feel I should explain why I told Paula that she could no longer be in the band." He was folding and unfolding his program in nervous agitation. "You see, she missed thirteen band practices in a month without any excuse except that she had other things to do. She was quite good on the flute, but I couldn't let one student constantly flout the rules or—"

"You don't have to justify it to me, Rich," Maggie interjected quickly. The poor man was a nervous wreck! She was infuriated with Greg for putting them through this.

"It was an unpleasant incident," Rich mumbled. "Dr. Wilder was furious with me."

"Yes, I know how unpleasant Dr. Wilder can be," Maggie said. They sat glumly as the drums began to roll.

Ten minutes later Max appeared at their feet. "Hi, Maggie!" He grinned at her, his face smeared with chocolate. He had crawled under the rows of seats to reach her and his hands and corduroy pants were filthy from the floor. Max dug deep into his pocket and pulled out an unwrapped piece of candy with teethmarks in it. "Want a Starburst Fruit Chew, Maggie?"

"Oh, Max," she sighed.

"I have to go to the bathroom," he announced, climbing into her lap. "Will you take me, Maggie?"

What choice did she have? Maggie asked herself as she walked Max to the bathroom. At four, he still consented to go into the ladies' room with her. She was furious with Greg, but it wouldn't be fair to take out her anger on an innocent child.

Max insisted upon sitting on her lap for the remainder of the concert. It was late, the child was tired, and his blood was probably running pure sugar after all that junk he'd eaten, Maggie reasoned, allowing him to stay with her. The last thing she wanted to risk was a volatile four-year-old's full-blown tantrum in the middle of the concert. Greg would undoubtedly remain in his seat and pretend he didn't know them, leaving her to cope alone. So Max sat in her lap in contented silence, popping candy into his mouth from the seemingly never-ending supply in his pockets.

Was it really only ten-thirty when the concert ended and the lights went on? Maggie felt as if she'd been sitting in the Civic Center for a full week with little Max in her lap and Rich Cassidy agitatedly twitching beside her. She'd spent the entire time watching and listening to the antics of the children five rows in front of her. She'd cringed every time someone in the audience hushed them with a disapproving glare. It didn't seem to bother Greg at all. He didn't even get upset when Kari stood on her seat and jumped off! Maggie's head was pounding as loudly as the drums by the time the audience rose and filed out.

"Mommy!" Kari called to her from the aisle. Maggie winced at the sight of her youngest child, who was a tangle-haired, grimy, candy-coated mess. "Mommy, Uncle Greg is taking us to the Ice Cream Emporium!"

Uncle Greg? Maggie was still reeling from that one when Max tore away from her to snake his way through the crowd. Maggie watched him land in the middle of the Wilder-May party. Greg caught her eye and gave her a brief mock salute. She didn't dare look at Rich Cassidy; she couldn't even begin to speculate on what he must be thinking.

Rich drove her straight home without saying a single word. Maggie tried to placate him with a heart-felt "I'm so sorry about this evening," but it didn't work. He merely grunted and did not walk her to her door.

Greg and the children didn't return for another hour. The irony of the situation was not lost on Maggie. She was home from her date and her children were out on the town with Greg Wilder. She heard them arrive a few minutes after midnight. Probably all of Woodland Courts did too. The Wilder children called noisy good-byes from the car as Kevin raced to the front door whooping. Greg carried a singing Kari on his shoulder and Kristin cartwheeled up the front walk. Maggie grimaced. All that sugar! She flung open the door and watched them, her hands on her hips.

"Hey, great concert, Maggie," Greg said as he set Kari on her feet with a flourish. "Loved those wood- winds and percussions."

"It isn't the least bit funny, Greg," she said icily.

Kari began to jump up and down. "We had so much fun, Mommy! We went to the Ice Cream Empo- rium and I had a banana split and an orange soda and—"

"Yes, I can see. You're wearing all of it," Maggie interrupted, glaring at Greg. "And it's a darn good thing I have a new bottle of Pepto-Bismol because all three of you are probably going to need it tonight."

"The kids are fine. Slap me five, Kevin." Greg held out his hand, palm up, and Kevin slapped it gleefully.

Maggie decided it was time to end the gaiety before she slapped Greg Wilder herself. And it wouldn't be on his palm. "Say good night to Dr. Wil- der, kids," she said briskly. "Kristin, will you run bath water for Kari? I'll be up in a few minutes."

"Sure. 'Night, Uncle Greg," called Kristin. "And thanks!"

"Thank you, Uncle Greg," chorused Kevin and Kari.

"It was my pleasure," Greg replied cheerfully. "Good night, kids." The children went inside and Greg turned to Maggie with a cocky grin. "They're great kids, Maggie. Thanks for letting me borrow them tonight."

Maggie's temper, suppressed during the long evening, erupted with volcanic force. Her face turned purple and her body trembled with fury. "Get out of here," she managed to say.

"It's too bad you didn't invite me inside," Greg said. "It would be so much more satisfying for you to throw me out of your house instead of merely off your doorstep."

"I don't want you in my house or on my doorstep," she said. "What you did tonight was unspeakable, Greg Wilder, and I—"

"Hi, Maggie!" Wendy, Josh, and Max called from the car. All three were hanging out the windows waving to her.

She felt compelled to respond with a wave and a cheery hello. She wasn't angry with the children; it wasn't their fault. But the brief interlude robbed her tirade of the necessary momentum. She tried to remember what she had been about to say.

"You were telling me how unspeakable I was tonight," Greg prompted. "And as much as I'd like to stay and listen, I'd better get the kids home to bed. It's getting late."

Maggie wasn't about to let him walk away without assuaging her rage. "Tonight was a complete fiasco," she hissed as he turned to walk to his car. "And it's—"

"So you didn't enjoy your first date as a single parent?"

"Enjoy it? It was a catastrophe! And—"

"A catastrophe?" he repeated. "That just about sums up most of my dates as well. We seem to have a lot in common, Mary Magdalene."

"Don't call me that! You deliberately set out to wreck my date tonight. I've never been so mortified in my entire life!"

"Are you sorry you went out with Cassidy tonight, Maggie?" he asked softly. "I told you that you would be. Maybe next time you'll listen to Uncle Greg."

"Ohh!" Maggie couldn't remember ever being so angry. The man had the power to infuriate her like no one and nothing else. "Why were you free on a Saturday night anyway? Wasn't your friend Lynn available tonight? After the *wonderful* time you had with her this afternoon, I'd have thought—" She broke off, horrified by her revealing transparence. Her temper had given her tongue free rein and she'd blurted out her jealous insecurities.

"Lynn?" For a moment Greg looked puzzled. Then he laughed. "I think you're referring to Chien and Ching Lin. The kids and I spent the afternoon with them. He's a radiologist at Hopkins and he and his wife threw a big birthday party for their little daughter Shirley today. It's an annual event, with both parents and children invited."

Maggie closed her eyes, aware that her face was somewhere between the shades of scarlet and crimson.

"You thought I'd spent the day with a woman named Lynn," Greg said jovially. "So that's why you're in such a stew, Green Eyes. Your catastrophic date with Cassidy has nothing to do with it!"

She had two choices, Maggie thought as she stood seething on the doorstep. She could stand there sputtering with impotent fury or she could exit grandly, slamming the door behind her. She opted for the latter.

Maggie spent a good portion of the night thinking of what she *should* have said to Greg Wilder when he so arrogantly sauntered to her door. Her revealing remarks about the mythical Lynn were never a part of the scenario, of course.

She was physically present with the children in church the next morning, but mentally she was annihilating Greg with a scathingly clever diatribe. In her imagination he was suitably chastened and pleading for her forgiveness. And she was cool and controlled and did not blurt out accusations like a juvenile, jealous fool. When the services ended,

Maggie was uncomfortably aware that she hadn't heard one word of the sermon.

"There's Uncle Greg's station wagon!" Kevin exclaimed as they rounded the bend into Woodland Courts. "Right in front of our house."

Maggie's stomach lurched. Kevin was right; the Wilders' long tan station wagon was parked directly in front of the duplex. Greg and his four children climbed out of the car as Maggie pulled her old Chevy into the driveway. Kevin, Kristin, and Kari bounced out of the car to greet them. Maggie stayed behind the steering wheel, trying to remember the brilliant rebuke she'd spent hours conceiving. Her mind seemed to have blanked at the sight of Greg walking toward her.

He opened the door of her car and extended a hand to her. Maggie ignored it and got out of the car by herself.

"I'm taking the kids boating today," Greg said, ignoring, in turn, her deliberate snub. "It'll probably be the last time we'll be taking the boat out this season. I'm on call next weekend and it will be too cold after that. We'd like you and the kids to join us, Maggie."

"No," she said automatically.

He frowned slightly. "I had a feeling you were going to say that, so I took out a little insurance."

"Mommy, Uncle Greg is going to take us on his boat!" cried Kari, rushing up to them. Maggie glared at Greg. His insurance was having his kids tell hers about the proposed outing. He didn't think she'd be able to say no to them.

"It's a big speedboat, Mom," Kevin said, joining them, his eyes alight with excitement. "Josh showed me pictures of it lots of times. I've always wanted to go on it."

Maggie felt trapped. "I really don't think—" she began, and all three of her children interrupted her with a desperate "Please, Mom!"

"Please, Maggie," Wendy said. Her beautiful

aquamarine eyes, so like Greg's, issued a plea of their own.

Max grabbed her around the knees and held on. "Please, Maggie!"

Greg was smiling smugly, quite pleased with his strategy. If she refused, she would be cast into the role of unreasonable spoilsport and he obviously didn't think she would accept that role.

Maggie had a surprise for him. "All right, you kids can go with Uncle Greg." She pronounced the name with delicate sarcasm. "But I have things to do today, so I'll stay home."

That was fine with the kids. They gave a cheer and ran into the duplex to change clothes. "Touché," Greg said softly, folding his arms across his chest. The action pulled the slick material of his navy windbreaker across his shoulders, emphasizing the hard muscles. He took a step toward her. He was wearing a pair of faded, well-worn blue jeans that seemed to be molded to the muscled columns of his thighs. He exuded a vital and forceful masculinity that both appealed and threatened.

Maggie swallowed and took a small step backward. Greg laughed softly. "Scared?" His gaze swept her body deliberately lingering on certain portions of her anatomy.

Sharp needles of sexual excitement pierced the pit of her abdomen. "Of you?" she said scornfully. "Why should I be? I beat you at your own game, Greg. Have a good time boating with the children today. It was most kind of you to invite them."

"Oh, you're coming with us, Maggie. Go inside and change into jeans and a sweatshirt or sweater. You have ten minutes."

"Do I?" She laughed at his arrogance. "Sorry, Greg. You lose this round."

"Unless you want to experience a little more of my caveman machismo, I suggest you go in and change, honey," he said silkily. "But then, maybe you do. You rather enjoyed that approach the last time, didn't you? I was so worried that I'd frightened shy little Maggie, but you loved it."

White-hot anger fueled by the sexual tension straining between them flared within her. She raised her hand, seeking a primitively feminine retribution. And caught herself in horror before she actually slapped his face.

"Go ahead, hit me," Greg taunted. "Then I'll have an excuse to retaliate. I'll kiss you senseless and then carry you straight to bed. Hell, that's what we both want anyway."

"No," she whispered. She was deeply shaken by the intensity of her emotions, and further unnerved by the realization that Greg was right. She was aching for a physical confrontation with him which would end . . . quite physically. It was more than a little frightening to have this volatile, passionate side of her nature revealed after years of seeing herself as calm, sensible, totally maternal. What had Greg Wilder unleashed in her? She stared at him, her green eyes reflecting her turmoil.

Paula Wilder chose that moment to make her acquaintance. "Hi, Mrs. May, I'm Paula." She approached Maggie with a friendly, curious smile. "I'm glad to meet you at last. We've talked on the phone so many times, I feel as if I know you already."

"Paula, will you please—" Greg began, but Maggie quickly interrupted him.

"I—I feel the same way, Paula," she said, striving to keep her voice from quavering. She felt as if she were on fire, that she was burning for Greg's touch, but she had to appear composed and dignified in front of his adolescent daughter.

Paula Wilder looked like the stereotypical fairy princess. A peaches and cream complexion, long white-blond hair swept up by two barrettes, light blue eyes fringed with the long dark lashes she'd inherited from her father.

There was a momentary silence as Maggie tried to

group her scattered wits. Greg continued to watch her with undisguised hunger blazing in his eyes.

"May I call you Maggie?" Paula asked pleasantly with a poise that the two adults were sorely lacking. "That's how I already think of you from hearing the kids talk about you all the time. And Daddy, too, of course," she added with a grin.

"Please do," Maggie managed with what she hoped was a warm smile.

"Paula, will you go check on Max?" Greg interrupted impatiently.

"Max is swinging on a tire swing in the back yard, Daddy. Kristin is with him."

"Then check on Wendy and Joshua," he ordered.

"They're both inside with Kari and Kevin," Paula reported.

"Then why don't you join them?" he said tightly. "Either out back or in the house. I'd like to talk to Maggie alone."

Maggie flushed, embarrassed by Greg's lack of subtlety and Paula's adultlike, knowing smile. "Paula, you're perfectly welcome to stay here," she said quickly, avoiding Greg's glittering eyes.

"Oh, no, I understand these things, Maggie," Paula assured her. "I have a boyfriend too." She walked off, tossing her long blond curls, her hips swaying provocatively in the tight blue jeans.

"What does she mean, she understands these things?" Greg was suddenly a befuddled parent. "She damn well better not!" He ran his hand through his hair. "You don't know what you have in store for you, Maggie. Kristin is still a little girl. Just wait until she hits adolescence." He shook his head, his expression glum. "My sweet little daughter has turned into a teenage version of Jekyll and Hyde. I never know what to expect from Paula these days."

The mother in Maggie felt strong empathy with the father in Greg. As a parent, he wasn't at all arrogant, challenging, or mocking. "It must be hard for you and for Paula without her mother," she ventured. "It's such a difficult time for a young girl."

"And this boyfriend business really has me worried. All of a sudden the boys in her class are too young for her. This kid she's seeing has his driver's license and his own car. I remember what I was like at his age and I sure as hell don't want my fourteen-year-old daughter to date a guy like that."

"It sounds like a situation that warrants close supervision, Greg."

"I know, I know, but it's damned difficult to practice medicine, look after three little kids, and keep an eagle eye on a headstrong teenager."

"I can imagine." Maggie laid her hand on his arm in an impulsive gesture of compassion.

Greg quickly covered her hand with his. "Come with us today, Maggie," he said huskily. "If you do, I might even apologize for sabotaging your date with Cassidy."

Somewhere along the line, her anger had been diffused. "You needn't have gone to all the time and expense," she admitted wryly. "The evening was rapidly sinking of its own accord before you and the kids ever appeared."

Greg grimaced. "Isn't dating ridiculous?"

"It's about as much fun as being mugged," she said. "Of course I'm not speaking from vast experience."

"I don't want you to have vast experience." He lifted her hand to his mouth and pressed her fingertips against his lips. "Maggie, I—"

"We're ready, Uncle Greg!"

"Let's go!"

"Mommy, you haven't even changed yet!"

"I'm hungry!"

All seven kids converged on them, everyone talking at once. Maggie quickly snatched her hand back. Greg groaned.

"Aren't you going to change clothes, Mom?" asked Kristin.

"You aren't still mad at Daddy, are you, Maggie?" Paula asked.

"She's not mad at him!" Kevin exclaimed, shocked by the very idea. "Why would she be mad at him?"

"For last night," Paula explained patiently.

"But we had a great time last night!" Kevin protested.

Paula's eyes met Maggie's and she smiled in amusement. She understood these things. Maggie looked at Greg. "We had a great time last night," he echoed, grinning.

All seven children were staring expectantly at her and Greg was smiling at her, a bold sexual challenge gleaming in his eyes. Maggie could feel her body responding to it, feel the tightening and the tension within. She wanted to tell him not to look at her that way, not to make her feel this way. Not in front of the children!

"Why don't you go inside and change your clothes while I load the kids into the car, Maggie?" Greg suggested. Before she could reply, he moved to stand closely behind her and gripped her arms. "Do you need any help getting undressed, sweetheart?" His voice was low in her ear, so low, only she could hear it. "Do you want me to help you with the zipper on your dress or the fastening on your bra or your panty—"

"No!" She jerked away, protesting the evocative images. Her pulses were throbbing. "It will only take me a few minutes to change," she said to the children in briskly bright tones. "I'll be right out."

She fled inside and only after she'd hurriedly changed into navy cords and a kelly green sweater did she realize how easily she had been manipulated. Because she had wanted to go all along? nagged a mocking little voice in her head. Maggie refused to answer on the grounds of self-incrimination.

Eight

The Wilders' boat was docked in Annapolis, which was a forty-five minute drive from Woodland. "We'll go down the Severn River and into Chesapeake Bay," Greg told them, and Paula pointed out the water route in the atlas.

The streets near the harbor in Annapolis were filled to overflowing with tourists, natives, and cadets from the nearby naval academy. The weather was crisp and clear, the October sun shining, and an almost holiday air seemed to prevail.

"Can we get ice cream cones before we go to the boat, Daddy?" asked Max, and Greg indulgently escorted them all into a crowded ice cream parlor where such exotic flavors as mango sherbet, brandy cordial, and butterscotch praline were offered. The conservative Mays and the cautious Wilders stuck with the traditional vanilla and chocolate.

"Now candy," suggested Max, veering into the doorway of a specialty candy shop.

"Absolutely not!" Maggie caught him and brought him back to the group on the sidewalk. "Not after that candy binge last night."

"Aw, gee, Mom," Greg said teasingly. "Nobody had to make use of your new bottle of Pepto-Bismol last night, did they?"

"No," she admitted. "But we're not going to press our luck. Deep-six the candy."

She means it, Uncle Greg," Kevin warned Greg seriously. "If we push her, she'll really get mad."

"Our sweet Mother Machree lose her temper? Never!" Greg said, but he steered the group past the candy shop and none of the children protested.

"Let's go into the toy store!" cried Josh, tugging at his father's arm and pointing to the tempting window display.

The latest shipment of a hard to obtain baby doll had just been unpacked and Kari dashed over to the shelf to grab a box containing a bald baby boy in a terry stretch suit. "Please, Mommy!" she gasped, breathless. "Please!"

"Don't you have one?" Paula asked curiously. "Wendy has three."

"Santa Claus couldn't bring me one." Kari clutched the box tightly. "Oh, please, can I have it, Mommy?"

Maggie wanted her to have it. She hadn't been able to lay her hands on the elusive doll last Christmas and had been depressed by her child's disappointment. But the cost of this doll was outrageous, no doubt jacked up for the free-spending tourist crowd. Maggie was shocked at the exorbitant price tag.

"Maybe there's a layaway plan, Mom," Kristin whispered. She wanted Kari to have the doll too.

"I'll buy you the doll, princess," Greg announced with a smile.

Kari's face was radiant and Maggie found it painful to intervene, though she knew she must. "No, Greg, I can't allow you to buy that doll for her. It's far too expensive for you to—"

"We can afford it," Paula broke in magnanimously.

"No," Maggie said firmly. She decided to inquire about a layaway plan. If she made a number of small payments over the next two months, she would have the doll by Christmas without putting an unmanageable dent in their budget.

"If you aren't going to buy that doll, I'll take it," a woman standing nearby said, reaching for the box. Kari hung on to it and stared mutely at the ground.

"Cry, Kari," advised Max in a loud whisper. "Scream."

"She'd better not," Maggie said. "Kari, honey, I know how much you want—"

She never got to finish. Kari was lifted right off her feet and swung into Greg's arms—doll, box, and all. He headed toward the cash register and Max and Wendy cheered their approval.

"Don't be upset, Maggie," Paula said. She stepped neatly in front of Maggie, blocking her path as she attempted to pursue Greg. "My father wants her to have the doll."

"I want her to have it, too, but I can't allow your father to spend that much money on her, Paula."

"Why not?" Paula moved at the same time Maggie did and short of shoving the girl aside, there was no way for Maggie to get around her. "If Daddy spent a lot of money on something for you—something like red roses—you wouldn't object, would you?"

Maggie's eyes flew to Paula's face and were met with an enigmatic smile. Exactly how much did Paula Wilder know about her father's romantic escapades, anyway? Maggie wondered, somewhat unnerved. "The question is moot, as he is *not* going to send me roses, Paula."

"I heard him order them this morning," Paula confided in a conspiratorial whisper. "They'll be waiting for you when you get home."

Greg had sent her roses? Maggie's heart did a queer little somersault. Paula winked at her and walked slowly away.

"Mom, look what Uncle Greg bought us!" Kevin's excited voice jarred Maggie from her state of bemusement. He was holding two small metal motorized cars, the kind he'd been wanting for ages and that

Maggie considered too pricey at eight dollars a car. "Maybe one for Christmas," she'd been saying for months. "Max and Josh and me each got two!" Kevin went on.

Maggie's jaw dropped. Greg was on a veritable spree! He was paying for a purple toy pony for Wendy when Maggie finally caught up with him. "I sent Paula and Kristin to that shop on the corner to buy earrings," he told her as he put his credit card back in his wallet. "They said they were too old for anything in here, although Kristin was eyeing that stuffed cat rather longingly. Shall I buy it for her?"

"No!" Maggie gasped. She linked her arm through his and half-dragged him from the shop. The kids trailed along, admiring each other's new toys.

"Mommy, this is the funnest day we ever had," Kari said. She'd already discarded the bulky box and was cuddling her doll in her arms. "Thank you, Uncle Greg," she added blissfully.

"You're welcome, honey." Greg looked pleased.

"Thanks a million, billion, trillion, Uncle Greg!" cried Kevin.

"Come on, gang, let's round up Paula and Kristin and get to the boat," Greg said eagerly.

"Wait a minute," Maggie said, troubled. "Josh, Wendy, Max, I didn't hear you say thank you to your daddy."

"You don't thank daddies," Max scoffed. "They're supposed to buy stuff for their kids."

"You always thank the person who gives you a present or does something nice for you," Maggie said. "Even if it is your daddy. *Especially* if it's your daddy," she added. "Will you try to remember that?"

"If we forget, you can remind us, Maggie," Wendy said. "Thank you for my pony, Daddy." Josh and Max chorused their thanks as well and all five dashed ahead to the corner store.

Greg turned to Maggie. "Thank *you*," he said, his eyes glowing with a warmth that made her breath catch in her throat.

"You're a wonderfully generous man, Greg," she said huskily. "Your own children should certainly learn to appreciate you."

He draped his arm around her waist. "I haven't bought anything for you today, Maggie. Let's—"

She took a deep breath. "Greg, please stop buying things for us!" she said. It was time to inject a note of reality into what was threatening to become a wonderful dream. "I'm keeping a running tab of what you've spent on my kids today and it will be the size of the national debt if you keep it up. I intend to reimburse you to the penny," she added firmly.

"Don't be ridiculous, Maggie. Ice cream, a few little toys . . . Do you really think I'd take money from you for that? I'm not going to let your prickly pride and outdated notions of propriety spoil the day. I enjoy treating the kids, both yours and mine. It gives me great pleasure to be able to do it."

"But—"

"You should always wear kelly green," he interrupted her. They had reached the corner and he drew her into the circle of his arms, seemingly oblivious to the throngs of people threading their way around them. "It makes your eyes shine like emeralds. Two bright sparkling emeralds."

Maggie felt her heart begin to race. She was mesmerized by the sensual line of his mouth, by the light in his own jewellike eyes. All time and place seemed to recede, leaving only Greg and her alone in this very private moment. His windbreaker was unzipped and her hands rested on his chest against the thick material of his blue cotton shirt. She longed to slip her fingers between the buttons and feel the wiry soft hair and warm skin and muscle within.

"I wish we were alone," Greg murmured, voicing her thoughts aloud. And then he took them one step further. "I wish we were naked in bed and I was inside you. I would—"

"Don't, Greg!" she pleaded as sensual heat surged through her. Her legs felt weak and it took considerable willpower not to melt against him. But she didn't dare, for their children were emerging from the shop and would soon be at their side.

"The frustration is killing me," Greg breathed against her ear. "It's natural for lovers to be completely engrossed and absorbed in each other. I want to shut out the rest of the world and lose myself in you, in us. But we have seven interested observers trying to be part of the act."

"They *are* a part of the act," Maggie said quietly, moving away from him. Her heart was hammering against her rib cage. Greg had called her his lover.

"I got sea gull earrings, Mom," Kristin said, eagerly showing her mother her purchase. "And so did Paula."

"You got the chartreuse lightning bolts too," said Paula, handing a small bag to Kristin. "I bought them for you. You were admiring them and Daddy gave me plenty of money."

"Thanks, Paula," exclaimed Kristin, stunned by her benevolence. "Thanks Dr.—uh—Uncle Greg."

"Our pleasure, right, Paula?" Greg said, beaming.

"Don't forget to say thank you to Daddy, Paula," Wendy piped up with a shy smile at Maggie. Maggie smiled back at her.

"Thanks, Daddy," said Paula.

Maggie's eyes met Greg's and a rush of pure happiness filled her. She was in love with him and, for this moment, that was enough.

"Can we go to the boat now, Daddy?" Josh asked impatiently.

"We're on our way. Let's go, crew," Greg called, taking Maggie's hand.

The boat was a thirty-four foot cabin cruiser with a powerful inboard motor that propelled the craft up to a speed of forty to fifty miles an hour. Greg gave each child, even the smallest ones, a turn at the wheel under his careful tutelage. Maggie relaxed in the front of the boat, admiring the passing scenery and enjoying the warmth of the sun on her face as they sped across the water. She was warmed by Greg's patient interaction with the children and by their exuberant high spirits. Kari was absolutely right, Maggie thought happily as the boat cut through the blue-green waters of the Chesapeake Bay. This was the "funnest" day they'd ever had.

"Would you like a turn at the wheel, Maggie?" Greg asked a long time later. She nodded, less interested in steering the boat than in sitting close to Greg, who hovered over each novice captain. She wasn't disappointed. Greg sat close beside her, his thigh pressing tightly against hers. Her head rested in the hollow of his shoulder and his heady masculine scent filled her nostrils. When he began to caress the nape of her neck lightly with his fingertips, a sensual shiver ran along her spine.

"We'll stay at my house tonight," Greg said lazily. "The kids can bed down two to a room and you and I can lock ourselves in my bedroom far from the madding crowd."

"We can't, Greg," she said breathlessly. It was difficult to think with his hand softly rubbing the sensitive skin of her neck. She was feeling the effects of his touch everywhere—in her taut nipples, in the pit of her stomach, between her thighs. . . .

"Of course we can." He leaned closer, his voice husky, his breath warm against her cheek. "You want to stay with me, don't you, love?"

Her eyelids fluttered. Why bother to deny the obvious? "Yes, but we—"

"Then there's no reason why we can't." His other hand dropped to close possessively around her thigh.

"There are seven very real reasons why we can't." She pried his fingers loose and placed his hand on the wheel. "Teaching children moral standards is difficult enough these days, Greg. What kind of an example would we be setting for our kids if we conducted a blatant affair right under the same roof?"

"You'd prefer a secret affair under a different roof?"

"That sounds tawdry too. Oh, Greg, I just can't go through with it. If I'd been thinking clearly, I'd have faced it from the start." She gave a small, mirthless smile. "But you have a way of making me not think at all."

"What are you trying to say, Maggie?" he asked harshly.

"Greg, I can't—"

"I'm getting cold, Mommy." Kari climbed across the seat to them. Greg and Maggie exchanged glances, their faces mirroring their mutual frustration at the interruption.

"We almost set a world record," Greg muttered. "We had nearly five full minutes to ourselves."

Kari was beginning to shiver. Maggie turned her full attention to her child. "You can sit on my lap, Kari. I'll hold you and keep you warm."

"I have an even better idea," said Greg. "Kari can drive the boat and I'll hold you on my lap, Maggie. You can keep *me* warm."

"Greg!" Maggie admonished, flushing.

"Oh, Uncle Greg!" Kari giggled. "You're so silly!"

"A better word would be desperate, Kari," Greg said as he shifted Maggie from her place behind the wheel to the seat beside him. He took over the steering as Kari plopped down on her mother's lap, the bald baby doll in her arms.

"It's getting late, we'll head back now," Greg announced to nobody in particular. "It'll be close to an hour before we're back in Annapolis."

"Hold me tight, Mommy," Kari ordered, snuggling in her mother's arms.

"Hold me too, Mommy." Max joined them, his face alight with mischief. He held his worn old bear under one arm and his two new cars in his hands. "Maggie," he corrected himself. "Mommy-Maggie." He and Kari both giggled.

"Is there room on my lap for Max too?" Maggie asked Kari.

The little girl paused to think. "Well, I guess so." She shifted to make a place for Max on her mother's lap. Wendy joined them next, squeezing herself between Greg and Maggie. "This is nice," Wendy said softly, leaning her head against Maggie's arm.

Greg gazed at Maggie and the three small children, then glanced to the back of the boat where the four older ones were laughing together. "Yes," he murmured thoughtfully. "It *is* nice, Wendy."

They docked the boat in Annapolis and Greg insisted on taking the whole group into one of the local seafood restaurants for dinner.

"I'd rather have hamburgers," grumbled Josh.

"I'd rather have pizza," added Paula.

"Fish!" Kari made a face. "Yuck!"

"Fish makes me throw up," warned Max.

"I have a terrific idea," Greg said with determined enthusiasm. "Why don't the seven of you go to that Italian restaurant up the street? You can stop at the hamburger stand along the way and get a burger for Josh. Maggie and I will eat here." He turned to her. "Unless fish makes you throw up?"

"Of course not, but do you—"

"Good!" Greg handed Paula several bills. "All of you, go! Order whatever you want and take your time eating."

"Fish doesn't make me sick, Uncle Greg," Kevin said. "I like it. I'll stay here with you."

"Kevin, we've just been politely told to get lost," Paula said with an air of exasperation. "They want to be alone. Now come on."

"How come they want to be alone?" demanded Max.

Kristin gazed thoughtfully at Greg and her mother. "They want to talk about boring grown-up things, Max," she explained, taking the little boy's hand. "We'll have a much better time having pizza."

Maggie saw Kristin and Paula exchange speculative smiles as they herded the younger children out the door. Their perception seemed much too adult and it bothered her. "Greg, I don't want the kids to know, uh, to think that—that . . ."

"That we're sleeping together?" Greg finished smoothly, guiding her to a cozy wooden booth in the corner of the restaurant.

She blanched. "We're not!"

"Sweetheart, we are. We slept together Friday night, we would have slept together last night if you hadn't been trying to prove your independence by going out with Cassidy, and we're going to sleep together tonight."

Maggie didn't know which point to refute first. "I wasn't *trying* to prove my independence, I am independent," she began hotly. "And we're not going to sleep together tonight!"

"Why not? You've admitted that you want to, Maggie."

"Well, we can't always do what we want," she retorted. "That's one of the first lessons taught by maturity."

"So . . ." Greg picked up the menu and appeared to study it. "You've decided not to see me anymore?"

A fierce pain jolted through her at the thought. "I didn't say that." Her reply was swift and vehement and she ducked behind her menu to hide her flushed face.

"Then you do want to see me." He stretched his long legs out under the booth, deliberately entangling her legs with his. "But you don't want to make love. You want a brother-sister type of relationship."

Maggie drew in her breath sharply. Her feelings for Greg Wilder were definitely not sisterly and she knew they never would be. "Greg, you're confusing me," she whispered nervously.

"I'm simply trying to define our relationship, Maggie. I'm as confused as you are."

Somehow, she doubted it. His eyes were focused intently upon her and he looked cool and calm and completely in control, while she was trembling, both inwardly and outwardly.

"Do you want to marry me?" he asked as casually as he might have inquired if she wanted the soup as an appetizer.

For a moment she was too shocked to speak. The room seemed to whirl and she gazed blankly at the menu. And then comprehension dawned. Greg was joking, of course. He expected her to come back with some witty rejoinder. None came to mind. It hurt too much to make jokes about dreams that could never come true.

"Well?" he prompted.

"Greg, I'm not really in the mood for jokes. I'm tired—all that wind and sun, I guess. Try me again tomorrow. I'll appreciate the humor then, I'm sure."

"I'm very serious, Maggie. I think we should get married."

She opened her mouth to speak but no words came out. At that moment the waiter arrived to take their order.

"Shall I order for you?" Greg asked politely. Maggie nodded. Had he guessed that she hadn't comprehended one printed word on the menu? Greg ordered a platter of Maryland crab cakes, cole slaw, and french fries for each of them. Having taken the order, the waiter departed, leaving them alone again.

"I can see I've taken you by surprise," Greg remarked dryly.

"I—I don't know what to say," Maggie stammered, and reached for her water glass. She took a gulp of ice water and promptly choked.

"You really are shaken, sweetheart. Does the idea of marrying me seem *that* farfetched to you?"

"I don't understand, Greg. You've known me for over two years and you've never displayed the slightest interest in—in marrying me, or anyone else for that matter. I'm the same person I was last week, last month—last year—and you never thought of marrying me then. What made you propose *now*?"

His lips curled into a sheepish, crooked smile. "Maybe I didn't realize until now that I'm madly and passionately in love with you."

She scowled at his attempt at humor. More than anything, she wanted those words—spoken jokingly, she knew—to be true. "That's funny, Greg." She made a strangled sound that was supposed to be a laugh. "Now tell me the real reason for this sudden proposal. If that really isn't a joke as well."

"I told you it's not a joke, Maggie." His voice deepened. "You don't believe that I want to marry you because I love you?"

"Not for a minute," she fired back.

"Then I have to assume that you're certainly not in love with me."

She didn't meet his eyes. He didn't love her, but she loved him. What if she were to admit her love to him? Would he then feel obliged to go through the motions of pretending to be in love with her? And would that be so bad? she wondered glumly.

"So we're not in love." Greg took her silence for assent. "However, that's no reason why we shouldn't marry, particularly when there are so many good reasons why we should." His piercing blue-green eyes seemed to pin her to her seat.

"Shall I list them for you, Maggie? We're both raising our children alone, and a two-parent family is more stable and secure. My kids need a mother and yours need a father. I think you're a wonderful mother and I want my children to have your love and care on a permanent basis. I'd do my best to be a good father to your children, too, Maggie. I already like them and I think they like me. And all seven kids seem to get along well enough, wouldn't you agree? Last, but certainly not least, our marriage would greatly improve your financial status. Think of that, Maggie. No more money worries. Ever."

"You make it sound like you're proposing a business merger, not marriage," she whispered. "You make it all seem so practical, so logical."

"It is practical. Logical too. I admire the way you've coped with your children and your life, Maggie. I respect you. And didn't today prove that we can function successfully as a combined family?"

Admire. Respect. Combined family. Maggie gazed at him bleakly. If only he loved her!

"Maggie, I like being married, I'm a family man." Greg leaned forward, his tone earnest. "These past two years have been a crazy aberration for me. I'm so sick of dating and meaningless small talk and unfamiliar bedroom rituals with different women. I want to spend my free time with my family, not chasing around like an overgrown adolescent. I haven't fared too well as a single parent, Maggie. Even when I preferred to be home, I felt a compulsion to go out. To me, a home and family are irrevocably bound up with having a wife."

"I see your problem," Maggie said wryly. "You want to spend your free time at home with your kids, but you also want sex. I can see where it would be convenient for you to have a wife safely stashed away in your bedroom for after the kids are tucked in for the night."

"I didn't mean to state it so badly. Sex is important to me, Maggie," he said bluntly. "You know I want you and you want me. The sexual chemistry is good between us but I wouldn't be marrying you strictly for sex.

"Honey, I would be a good husband to you," he continued in an urgent, low voice. "I would be a good provider, I would be faithful to you and—and I would try never to hurt you."

His words swirled around surrealistically in Maggie's head. A good provider. He would see to it that she and her children had food, clothing, and a roof over their heads. The government and any number of charitable institutions would do the same. He would be faithful to her because it would be convenient for him; he'd already made it clear that he was tired of changing beds on weekends. He cared about her—as a mother, a person, a friend. That was the way she felt toward her next-door neighbor. And he claimed he would try never to hurt her? He was killing her right now! Every word seemed to pierce her heart like the blade of a dagger.

The waiter brought their food. Greg devoured his dinner with relish; Maggie picked listlessly at hers. "I think we should get married as soon as possible," he said as he polished off his crab cakes. She offered him her second one and he accepted it at once. "I'm on call next weekend, but the weekend after that would be fine. After all, why wait?"

Why, indeed? Maggie thought later. Greg didn't even wait for her to give him her answer. He assumed that the wedding was a foregone conclusion and announced the marriage to all seven children as they drove home. Maggie was stunned, furious, and close to tears. The kids were so happy! Kevin, Kristin, and Kari were all ready to call Greg Daddy. Max, Wendy and Josh wanted to call her Mommy.

"Now we can get a baby like Nicole," Kari said happily.

"It better be a boy baby," argued Josh. "I don't need any more sisters."

"Well, I don't need any more brothers," Wendy said boldly. "I want a baby sister." Maggie was too chagrined to take pleasure in the little girl's uncharacteristic defiance of her brother.

"Maybe they can have a boy *and* a girl," Kevin said tactfully. "Then everyone will be happy."

"Oh, sure." Greg chuckled, and reached for Maggie's hand. "What do you think, sweetheart? There are four of mine and three of yours. Shall we have at least one of ours?"

Maggie paled. The man was mad! And a manipulating conniver as well. By telling the children of his insane plan, she would be placed in the awful position of dream-wrecker when she refused to comply.

"I'm very happy that you're going to marry my father, Maggie," Paula said in that dulcet voice of hers. "I'm so tired of baby-sitting for the kids on weekends while he goes out on dates. Now you can both stay home and I can go out with my friends."

"I'm not marrying Maggie to gain a live-in baby-sitter, Paula," Greg admonished her.

"Oh, I know that, Daddy," she replied blithely. "You want a live-in date too. Now you'll have both."

And what would she have? Maggie wondered morosely. Four more children and a husband who didn't love her. The mind-boggling possibility of an eighth child! A live-in date and baby-sitter combination, eh? She decided then and there that she would hold onto her independent status as a *paid* sitter and refuse Greg's bloodless, practical, logical proposal.

Greg braked to a stop in front of 909 Woodland Courts. "Will you keep the kids after school tomorrow?" he asked above the hubbub of children's voices. "I'll try to leave the hospital a little early and we'll all go out for a celebration dinner."

"Can we go to Chuck E. Cheese?" Max asked hopefully.

"That would be romantic," Paula said sarcastically.

"It wasn't quite what I had in mind either," Greg agreed, laughing. "Now all Mays out of the car. Wilders wait here while I walk Maggie to her door."

"And kiss her good night," drawled Paula, who knew about these things.

"Gross!" Josh said.

"When you marry Mommy, will we be Wilders too?" asked Kari, skipping between Greg and Maggie on the short walk to the door.

"I'd be happy for you to use my name, Princess," Greg replied in a warm, paternal voice. "We'll talk it over with Mommy later."

"Kevin Wilder," Kevin said, throwing away his May heritage without a moment's hesitation. "I like it."

"Greg!" Maggie said, her teeth clenched together. "I want to talk to you. Right now!"

"Kristin, take Kevin and Kari inside, dear," Greg said, playing Daddy again. "Your mother will be along in a minute."

" 'Night, Dad!" Kevin cried exuberantly. Kari insisted on giving Greg a hug and a kiss. At first Kristin hung back shyly, but she finally found the nerve to place a quick peck on Greg's cheek.

"Well, now you've really done it!" Maggie said, turning on him furiously after the children had gone inside. "What am I supposed to tell those children now, Greg Wilder?"

"That we're getting married in two weeks, that I'll be their new daddy, and that we'll all live happily ever after."

"Except that we won't! You never gave me an opportunity to reply to your proposal, Greg, so I'll do so now. My answer is no! I'm not going to marry you."

"Of course you are, honey. You're just having a case of bridal nerves. What scared you, Maggie? Was it the talk about having another baby? I was just having a little fun with the kids. If you don't want another child we won't have one, it's as simple as that."

"Having another baby has nothing to do with it! Greg, you had no right to tell the kids we were getting married! I didn't say I'd marry you. I haven't said it yet and I'm not going to!"

"Daddy, hurry up," Joshua shouted from the car. "Max has to go to the bathroom."

Greg glanced from Maggie to the car. "I'll take the kids home and be back within an hour. We'll talk then."

"If by talk you mean that you intend to bulldoze me into saying yes, then don't bother, Greg. I won't be rushed into anything that—"

"Sooner or later you're going to marry me, Maggie," he interrupted impatiently. "If not for my money, then to legalize our affair. So why prolong the inevitable?"

She felt as if she'd been punched in the solar

plexus. "I would never marry for money! And we aren't going to have an affair!"

"We're having one now, Maggie, and you don't want your children or mine to know about it. If you turn down my proposal, I can only assume that you'd prefer an open affair. And it will be open, baby. Our children and the entire community of Woodland will know that we're sleeping together, I promise you that."

"You're not going to threaten me, Greg Wilder!"

"Threaten you? Darling, I'm trying to propose to you. We'll talk later," he promised in maddeningly soothing tones. "I'll be back after I take the kids home."

"I won't let you inside!"

"You can't relegate me back to the doorstep, sweetheart." He laughed, a soft dangerous laugh that sent a little chill along her spine. "I've already been inside. Inside your house, inside your life, inside you, Maggie. You can't keep me out and I think you know it." He dropped a light kiss on her forehead. "I'll see you in an hour or so."

She'd only been home for a few minutes when Mrs. Jenkins arrived from her half of the duplex, carrying a ceramic vase with a dozen long-stemmed red roses in it. "The florist come to deliver them this afternoon, and since you weren't here, I took them in for you," Mrs. Jenkins explained. "I put them in water. They do look lovely in this vase, don't they? It's one of my favorites."

"Yes, thank you, Mrs. Jenkins." Maggie stared at the roses, slightly overwhelmed. "They're beautiful. No one has ever sent me roses before."

"Red roses traditionally mean love and romance." Mrs. Jenkins sighed. "Here's the card." She handed Maggie a small sealed envelope. "Did Dr. Wilder send them? I believe he spent Friday night here."

The envelope fluttered from Maggie's hand and she stooped to retrieve it. Oh, no, it was beginning already—gossip linking her and Greg. An open affair, he had said. They'd slept together one night and Mrs. Jenkins knew about it. In another day or so, all of Woodland Courts would know too. "Mrs. Jenkins, how—how did you know?"

"I go to bed very late and get up very early. I saw his car both times." Mrs. Jenkins shook her head at Maggie's stricken face. "I'm not condemning you, Maggie dear. No one knows better than I how sterile your life has been for the past six years. I'm delighted you've found a gentleman friend."

"He's asked me to marry him," Maggie blurted out. For reasons no doubt buried deep in her psyche, she simply couldn't bear to have her neighbor think her relationship with Greg was merely a casual liaison.

"Oh, Maggie, how wonderful!" Mrs. Jenkins's face lit up. "A rich doctor! How wonderful for the children! I'm so happy for all of you!"

Maggie winced. A rich doctor. Mrs. Jenkins thought she'd climbed aboard the gravy train. Everyone in Woodland Courts would think the same. She'd managed to snag a wealthy husband; she was moving up and out. Her fiery Irish pride rebelled at the notion. Dammit, she'd managed to survive and provide a decent living for herself and her kids. She was no Cinderella waiting around to be rescued by the wealthy prince! "But I haven't decided whether or not to accept his proposal," she said, setting her jaw.

"Oh, Maggie!" This time Mrs. Jenkins's expression was one of pure dismay. "What's to decide? Rich doctors who will take on a widow with three children don't grow on trees, you know. I'd say marry him as soon as possible."

Mrs. Jenkins and Greg seemed to be in perfect agreement on that, Maggie thought. For different reasons, or course. Greg wanted her baby-sitting and sexual services on a more convenient basis; Mrs. Jenkins thought she should take no chances in securing ownership of the golden goose. Neither cared at all that what Maggie would be getting was a husband who didn't love her.

Nine

The children chattered incessantly and excitedly as they got ready for bed. Maggie assumed she must have given them the correct responses, but she barely heard a word that was spoken. She was too preoccupied with her own thoughts. What if she married Greg? What if she didn't? At this point in time she couldn't seem to envision either course of action. She slipped into her long pale blue nightgown. What was she going to do?

The doorbell rang and she froze. She wasn't ready to face Greg. She needed more time to think, to shore up her defenses. She could do neither in the potent presence of Greg Wilder.

"Ready for bed already?" he said when she answered the door. His amused eyes swept over her nightgown-clad figure. "That's fine with me, love, although I thought we were going to have coffee and talk first."

Maggie cursed herself for forgetting to put on a robe and slippers. This was the first time in her adult life that she'd ever answered the door wearing only her nightie! Greg had her so shook up that she couldn't seem to follow a coherent train of thought. "The kids are still awake," she said tersely. "I'd appreciate it if you dropped the not-so-veiled innuendoes."

"The lady's wish is my command."

"Would you like to come in?" she asked with frozen hauteur.

Greg gave a low whistle. "Will wonders never cease! She actually *invited* me inside. And all it took was a proposal of marriage."

Maggie refused to acknowledge the joke. "You said you wanted coffee," she said sternly. "You can hardly drink it on the doorstep. Although you shouldn't drink coffee at all at this time of night. The caffeine will keep you awake all night and I don't have any decaffeinated coffee to offer you."

"Sweetheart, I *plan* to be awake a good part of the night." He caught her round the waist and hauled her back against his chest. His lips brushed the soft skin along the curve of her neck and Maggie felt something akin to a bolt of electricity shoot through her. When his hands moved upward with slow confidence to cup her breasts, she drew a long, ragged breath. She'd been waiting all day for this, she admitted to herself. She craved his touch.

"Why don't we skip the coffee?" Greg's husky voice made her pulses throb. "I don't need the caffeine as a stimulant, darling. You're ten times as potent."

"Mommy?" Kari appeared at the head of the stairs, seemingly out of nowhere.

"Uh-oh," said Greg. "Caught in the act. Well, almost."

Kari stared intently at the sight of her mother in Greg's arms. Maggie tried to wriggle free, but Greg didn't release her. He removed his hands from her breasts but continued to hold her firmly against him. "What are you doing out of bed, princess?" he asked pleasantly.

"I heard the doorbell and I thought it was my new daddy. I wanted him to tuck me in," Kari said.

"Your new daddy would love to tuck you in, Kari." Greg released Maggie and loped up the stairs, two steps at a time. He swooped Kari up in his arms and carried the giggling little girl into her room.

Maggie heard him talking to all three children,

heard the good nights and the laughter and Kari's plea for one more hug. Her children were starved for a man's attention. Why hadn't she recognized that fact until now? It was so obvious that Greg's children needed a mother. How had she managed to remain oblivious to her own children's acute need for a father's love?

Lost in thought, she walked slowly into the kitchen to put on the coffee. It was beginning to perk when Greg joined her. "I had a nice talk with the kids," he said, making no attempt to resume the lovemaking preliminaries that had been interrupted. "They're great kids, Maggie. You've done a wonderful job with them."

Maggie glowed in spite of herself. The one sure-fire way to reach her was through her children.

"I see you got the roses." Greg watched her pour the coffee into two mugs and carry them to the table, along with the sugar bowl and a carton of milk. The roses were sitting in the middle of the table in Mrs. Jenkins's vase.

"My neighbor was wildly impressed." Maggie sat down at the table and poured a little milk into her coffee. "She thinks I should jump at the chance to marry you. Tomorrow isn't too soon for her."

"You told her I asked you to marry me?"

Too late Maggie realized what she'd given away. "She—she saw your car here all night Friday." She sipped her coffee. It was hot and rich and seemed to strengthen her. And she remembered her manners. "Thank you for the roses, Greg," she said primly. "They're lovely."

"Come over here and thank me properly," he said challengingly, and laughed when she didn't move from her chair. "Never mind, I can wait until later when you're not feeling so shy."

She jumped up from her chair, at once restless and excited and aroused. Greg controlled her as easily as a puppet on a string, she admitted to herself. A look, a touch, or a few words from him could make her feel exactly what he wanted her to feel. She sought to break the invisible strings by focusing on some mundane domestic task.

"I'm hungry. I'm going to make some toast." She carefully turned her full attention to the task. "Would you like some?"

"No thanks." Greg watched her work for a few minutes. And then, "Maggie, how did Johnny die? You've mentioned several times that he was killed, but I've never heard the full story."

His question caught her by surprise. She assumed everyone who knew her knew the facts surrounding Johnny's death. She hadn't told the story in years, for her neighbors, who knew all the facts, were quick to pass them along to newcomers to Woodland Courts.

"Johnny was a policeman on the Baltimore police force," she began, and Greg nodded. He knew that. "And he was shot and killed by the man driving the getaway car in a bank robbery in the city. Kari was just a week old at the time." She added that last for no other reason than that she always did when she discussed Johnny's death. The two facts were irrevocably bound in her mind. The local news had focused on it too during the brief time that Officer John May's death was a front-page story.

"It must have been a terrible time for you," Greg murmured.

"Of course, you know what it's like." Maggie stared into space. "The phone call that changes your life forever and turns an ordinary day into a living nightmare. The traumatic adjustment to an irreplaceable loss. The days when you go through the motions of living and wonder why. You've been through it all too."

Greg nodded grimly. Although Maggie knew the circumstances of Alicia's death, he wanted to share them with her. "A drunk driver hit Alicia's car and pushed it into the path of a truck in the passing lane. The car was totaled and she was pronounced dead at the scene."

"I remember hearing the news on the radio," Maggie said softly. "I was stunned. I couldn't believe it had happened to little Joshua Wilder's mother, the lovely woman that I knew."

"I felt so helpless, Maggie. As a neurosurgeon, I'd been able to save accident victims with head injuries, but there wasn't a thing I could do for my own wife."

"And then comes the anger, the rage," added Maggie, remembering. "It took me a long time to work through that."

"It was the same for me. And I'm still a little irrational on the subject of drunk drivers."

"I'll never feel kindly toward bank robbers either," she said wryly. And added quickly, "I didn't mean to sound flippant, Greg. I was just—"

"I know, honey." His voice was kind. "I know."

She felt that he really did understand and was touched by the moment of shared compassion and mutual understanding. "Greg, how long after Alicia's death did you begin to date?" She was very curious; she'd often wondered about it.

"I assume we're both using the word 'dating' as a euphemism for taking a woman to bed?" Greg gave a slight laugh. "I had sex for the first time four months after Alicia was killed. It didn't mean anything, no emotions or feelings were involved at all. I think I just wanted to know if I was still alive. An existential pinch on the arm, so to speak. And it's continued along that vein."

Maggie said nothing, but her heart was sinking fast. She wished she hadn't asked. To her, Greg's lovemaking had been passionate and deeply fulfilling, an affirmation of life and love. But to him it had been merely an existential pinch on the arm? She felt sick.

"Maggie, during the past six years, didn't you ever want, wonder . . .?" His voice trailed off.

She shrugged. "Working all night, taking care of kids and the house during the day, and trying to grab some sleep whenever I had a spare moment was my existential pinch on the arm, I guess."

She ate her toast and they finished their coffee in silence. Maggie wondered what Greg was thinking. He was studying her with an intensity that she found unnerving. Was he remembering Alicia and comparing her to his beautiful and beloved wife? Was he regretting his impulsive proposal, wondering how to withdraw it? She had no idea and she was afraid to ask. Afraid to hear his answer, she realized with uncomfortable insight.

At last Greg glanced at his watch. "Do you think the kids are asleep yet?"

"Probably." She carried the empty mugs and her plate to the sink. "They were worn out. Kari took her new doll to bed with her and—"

"Good. Glad to hear it." He was on his feet and his hand snaked out to seize her wrist. He was staring at her with a fixed intensity. Maggie realized the reason for his seemingly innocuous question a little too late.

Greg confirmed her supposition. "Let's go to bed, Maggie."

Just like that, she thought. Let's go to bed, Maggie. Had he decided that although she was no match for Alicia, at least she was available? Her temper flared. Dammit, she was no one's existential pinch on the arm. "No, Greg."

"Yes, Maggie," he said, mimicking her tone. "We both need it, honey. We've been alternately aching, burning, and frustrated all day long."

"Not me!" she said with such vehemence that Greg laughed. They both knew she was lying.

"Sweetheart, I'm not going to stand here and argue with you." Greg swept her up into his arms and walked briskly out of the kitchen.

"Put me down!" she said, gasping. She was aware that her body was clamoring for him to ignore her indignant demand. And ignore it he did, murmuring something outrageously and blatantly sexual in her ear as he carried her up the stairs.

In a matter of seconds they were in her bedroom and the door was locked. Greg set her on her feet but kept her in his arms. His gaze fastened on her mouth, and her lips parted and tingled, as if he had physically touched her. When his gaze lowered to her breasts, her nipples grew hard and tight, responding to his sensual scrutiny with a will of their own. "Maggie, my darling, my love," he said thickly. "I want you so badly."

The undisguised hunger in his voice touched a cord deep within her. She wanted him with the same intense urgency.

His hands closed possessively over her breasts and they swelled beneath his fingers, fingers that kneaded and stroked and made her moan with pleasure. He claimed her lips, thrusting his tongue into her mouth at the same moment that he inserted his thigh between hers. The double mastery was shattering. The hot, dull ache in her abdomen erupted like a blazing volcano, sending spurts of hot lava coursing through her veins.

Maggie felt a deep and primitive need to surrender to Greg, yet at the same time she was filled with the desire to possess *him*, to drive him out of himself and into her loving power. Existential pinch on the arm? Tonight she would make Greg Wilder forget everyone and everything but the passion burning between them. She wanted him out of control with need of her. Tonight he would be acutely aware that both of them were very much alive.

"Are you aching for me now, Greg? Are you burning for me?" she demanded huskily. She undressed quickly and he watched her with glazed, hungry eyes. Standing naked, she wrapped her arms around his neck and kissed him, moving her body sinuously against his.

Greg tugged off his shirt and fumbled clumsily with his belt buckle. Maggie felt a thrilling sense of feminine power at the sight of his unsteady hands. "Let me," she whispered, and brushed her knuckles lightly over his thrusting masculinity before lowering the zipper with erotically slow precision. His uncontrollable response to her was enthralling. A pulsing excitement rippled through her when he moaned her name.

Emboldened, she pulled him over to the bed and pushed him down to sit on the edge. She climbed onto his lap, feeling the hardness of his hair-roughened thighs under her. Her hands moved over the satisfying solidity of his chest, over the whip-cord muscles of his arms to the smooth length of his back. It was intoxicating to touch him like this, to feel his fierce masculine response to her.

"Maggie, Maggie, I need you so," he said urgently.

"Not yet," she teased, delicately sinking her teeth into an earlobe. "I'm not ready yet."

"Then I'm going to have to make you ready, sweetheart, because I can't wait any longer."

His hand closed over her bare breast and began a slow, sensuous massage while his fingers played with her nipple, arousing it to aching sensitivity. His mouth closed over it and he began to suck with a firm erotic rhythm. Maggie felt the effects deep within her womb and whimpered with pleasure.

"Now, darling?" His fingers slipped between her thighs to probe the moist warmth there. "You're hot and flowing and ready for me. Let me have you now, love."

Maggie trembled as his fingers teased and stroked with sensual expertise. "Kiss me, Greg," she breathed, and his mouth clamped over hers with greedy possession. Their tongues met and dueled hotly. Greg lay back on the bed, carrying her with him, their mouths still fused together. But when he would have rolled her on her back and moved on top of her, she slipped away from him.

"Still not yet, Greg," she said in a husky tone. "First I want to feel and taste every inch of you." Her tongue traced the outline of his hard nipples, then dipped into the hollow of his navel.

"Maggie," he groaned in protest. "Sweetheart, I don't think I can wait any longer."

She gazed languidly into his eyes. "Every inch, Greg darling." Her lips teased his pulsating strength. His control started to slip and she heard him call out her name, but she wouldn't relinquish her power. Then she felt his control completely lapse, felt the life force flow from him, and knew that in this moment at least, Greg was all hers and passionately alive with feeling.

"Why did you do it?" he asked huskily some moments later, pulling her up to him. His blue-green eyes were ablaze. "You deliberately teased me and wouldn't stop until—"

"I thought you needed a lesson," she replied succinctly, grinning her triumph. "And I decided to give it to you."

"So you want to play sexual games?" Her glee subsided somewhat as she stared into the dark intensity of his eyes. "It's you who needs a lesson, Mary Magdalene, and I'm going to be the one to teach it to you."

For the next few hours, Maggie learned lessons in passion and arousal, in power and control and helpless ecstasy. Greg was a skilled and thorough teacher, combining sexual expertise with calculated control to arouse her again and again to the peak of throbbing, frustrated desire. Just as she felt herself beginning to slip over some invisible edge, just as every nerve tightened and focused on the hot inner pulsing, Greg would withdraw and make her plead for completion. Time after time, made helpless and vulnerable by his passionate onslaught, she would beg him to stop, only to reverse herself and plead with him to go on. And each time she spun wildly and vividly out of control, he would reward her by taking her to the heights of rapture.

She couldn't get enough of him. She felt as if she had crossed some great divide. Greg had exposed a facet of herself that she had never dreamed existed, had exposed herself to *her*. Beneath the controlled asexual madonna that she'd thought she was, slumbered a passionate woman who craved, *demanded*, her man's passion in return. She wanted to give and give to Greg, but she wanted to take too. It was an illuminating lesson.

She felt sensual and unfettered and free, released from all pressure, all control. In bed with Greg she could always let go, she realized with newfound insight. She loved and trusted him. He allowed her to be both a woman and a mother. He had fused her separate halves and made her whole.

A long, long time later Maggie lay in Greg's arms, a blissful lethargy creeping through her, her body warm and damp and pliant beneath his hands. "Greg," she whispered lovingly. Tears filled her eyes and emotion surged through her as she gazed into his beautiful eyes. She hoped their baby would have his eyes.

She was so in love with him, she thought. She would marry him and raise his children along with hers, and give him a baby, their own child. And if he didn't love her yet, she was certain that eventually he would. He was a family man, he liked being married. It was inevitable that he would fall in love with the woman who was his wife. Maggie wondered why she'd been too dense to realize that earlier. There was a lot she had learned tonight.

She rolled onto her stomach, deliciously drowsy. The clock read three A.M., making it already Monday morning. In just a few hours she would have to get the kids up for school. The thought made her groan.

"Oh, God, Maggie," Greg said with dismay. "What have I done to you?"

He'd seen her tear-moist eyes, and when he'd heard the small sound of discomfit and seen her roll away from him, he'd gone rigid. What *had* he done? For the past few hours he had been in a passionate frenzy, governed by some inexplicable masculine need to prove to Maggie that she belonged to him and always would. Never had he engaged in such primitive and uncontrolled passion, never had he made such demands. And she had been with him all the way, taking everything he had to give and demanding more, giving herself to him in unbridled surrender. Because he had forced her?

With his raging passion assuaged, Greg faced the question with rational and unnerving logic. Maggie was a fiercely proud and independent woman and he had made her admit her need for him in the most elemental way. Could she forgive him for that? She had ceded all control to him and lost herself in the heat of passion. Was she hating him for it? Was she fearful that the primitive male dominance he had asserted in bed would spill over into their life together and that he would tyrannize and repress her? The thought appalled him. He wasn't a physical type who used his strength to dominate. Like most neurosurgeons, he considered himself rather cerebral, using his intellect and skill over actual physical strength to win his victories. Never in his wildest fantasies—which had always been rather tame, he realized now—could he have envisioned a night like tonight, with himself in the swashbuckling, passionate hero's role. He'd felt as triumphant as one of his Cro-Magnon ancestors who'd won the woman of his choice by dragging her into his cave. He'd felt exultant, rejuvenated, and deeply in love. And then he had seen the tears in Maggie's eyes.

She was lying on her stomach, her face on the pillow, her eyes closed. Her breathing, at first shallow and erratic, was gradually becoming deep and even. He laid his hand on the silky warmth of her back and couldn't resist tracing the beautiful, straight line of her spine with his finger. A potent combination of pride and love and possession filled him. She was his.

"Maggie?" he whispered.

She didn't open her eyes. "You teach one helluva lesson, Dr. Wilder," she said in a thick, sleepy voice. When there was no responding chuckle, she opened one eye with great effort. Greg was staring down at her, his face shadowed with worry and concern.

Maggie felt she knew him so well now, she could read his mind. "Greg, go home to the children." She knew he didn't want to leave her tonight, but his parental obligation to his children would be weighing heavily on his mind. Hopefully, he didn't fear she would throw a tantrum like those unreasonable women he'd been dating. No, he wouldn't expect such behavior from her, she assured herself. He knew her as well as she knew him. And he must know that although she wanted him to stay all night, she recognized his paternal concern. And respected him for it, loved him for it. "Go home, Greg."

She was kicking him out! Greg thought, aghast. He had overwhelmed her, had hurt and scared her. And now she was telling him to leave! "Maggie, we have to talk." His voice shook. He would soothe and explain and apologize, whatever it took.

Maggie smiled to herself, an inward smile, for she was too exhausted, too marvelously replete to expend the energy to move the necessary facial muscles. "I couldn't talk now if my life depended on it, Greg." It was supposed to be the man who rolled over and fell into dead slumber afterward, she thought with drowsy amusement as sleep rolled over her in waves. She and Greg could have a good laugh about it tomorrow. But now . . . Her thoughts drifted off. She couldn't stay awake another second.

She wouldn't even talk to him! Greg was distraught. "Maggie?" She didn't answer him. She was pretending to be asleep. He knew only too well how adept she was at shutting him out. He felt himself begin to panic. "Darling, I love you," he tried on an anguished note. But there was still no response from her. "Sweetheart, please! Don't do this to us. We can talk it out. I—"

She rolled over on her side, her eyes still closed. Her breathing was even and deep and she was doing a masterful job of feigning sleep. Because she hated him and wanted him to go away, Greg reminded himself bitterly.

He dressed quickly and left the bedroom with a last despairing glance at her still form. She still hadn't agreed to marry him, he remembered on the lonely, cold drive back to his house. She didn't love him and didn't believe he loved her. And after experiencing his savagely possessive performance tonight, she probably never would.

Common sense told him that it had been too soon to propose marriage. Maggie was only now beginning to emerge from the protective shell she'd withdrawn into after the shock and pain of her husband's traumatic death. Her passionate nature was starting to reawaken after the long period of dormancy. The very thought of her entering the world of singles dating made Greg break out in a cold sweat. He hadn't really viewed the hapless Rich Cassidy as a threat, but the idea of her dating other men, of being subjected to their charms and wiles and sexual demands, had driven him to stake a possessive claim upon her. And after he had taken her to bed, he'd wanted to insure his claim, to bind her to him legally and morally and any other way there was.

Marriage had been the only logical solution. But he should have waited, Greg chastised himself glumly. She'd been incredulous at the idea, totally unable to believe that he loved her. Because, he knew, she didn't love him. Once they were safely married, he was sure he could make her fall in love with him, but he needed the exclusivity and opportunity marriage would provide to woo her properly. Conducting a courtship with seven omnipresent children was a virtual ticket to the madhouse. He needed the legally sanctioned privacy of marriage to win Maggie's love and trust.

When she'd said no, he hadn't wanted to believe it. He knew he was wrong to tell the kids, but he was beyond fighting fair. And now . . . Greg walked slowly into the big house that seemed empty and lifeless to him. He hadn't thought of it as home in two years. When he and Maggie married, they would buy a new house, one they had chosen together. When they married . . . Greg lay down on his bed, still fully dressed. If they married . . .

Ten

When the alarm clock went off at seven o'clock, Maggie hopped out of bed with surprising energy, given her few hours of sleep. She felt marvelous and hummed to herself as she showered and dressed and performed her other morning ablutions. She chose her brightest outfit, a cheery canary-yellow corduroy skirt and vest teamed with a white blouse. The bright color matched her mood.

She made bacon and eggs for the kids' breakfast and jollied them out of their Monday morning grumpiness. At school she had a smile for everyone. It was gray and raining outside, but to Maggie the world had never looked more beautiful. She was in love and she was going to marry the most generous, kind, understanding, and *sexy* man in the whole world.

Not even a telephone call at noon from the Woodland Children's Center dampened her spirits. "I'm calling you because we can't reach Dr. Wilder," came the nasal voice of the director of the center," and we know you are Max's baby-sitter, Mrs. May. Max is running a temperature of one hundred and three. Our policy is not to accept a child with an elevated temperature. He'll have to leave."

Maggie frowned. "You want me to take him?"

"We can't reach Dr. Wilder. He is supposedly in surgery," the director intoned, as if she didn't quite believe it. "We can't keep a sick child here and risk exposing the other children. If you don't take Max, I'll have to call Woodland Family Services and refer the problem to them."

"Max is not a problem," Maggie replied coolly. "I'll be right over to pick him up."

The principal wasn't too thrilled when Maggie told him she was leaving and would be gone for the rest of the day. But it was certainly simpler to call the district office and get a replacement for her than to rout Greg from surgery. Maggie faced the situation realistically and without resentment. Max needed her. And Greg needed her to be with his child. She assumed the role with loving acceptance.

Poor Max was hot and listless, and he curled against her in the front seat of the car without saying a word. Maggie drove him directly to the Woodland Clinic, an outpatient facility used by Woodland residents and others who subscribed to the Woodland Medical Plan. Maggie wasn't sure if the Wilders did or not, but the receptionist in the pediatric clinic, whom she knew well, promised to slip Max in as a "drop-in."

They left ninety minutes later with a diagnosis of an ear infection and a prescription for a decongestant and an antibiotic, which Maggie had filled at the nearby Woodland Pharmacy. Once Max was settled in the cot in Kevin's room after a dose of the medicine and a glass of juice, Maggie tried to reach Greg.

He wasn't available and his receptionist wasn't exactly helpful about letting her know his whereabouts. She finally told Maggie that Dr. Wilder wasn't in his office or in surgery, but was somewhere in the hospital. She suggested Maggie have him paged there. As Maggie was placing the call it occurred to her that life as a doctor's wife wasn't going to be all that different from life as a policeman's wife. Both jobs involved unpredictable hours and emergencies; both called for her to make most of the decisions and take most of the responsibility for the children on her own. The prospect didn't frighten or disturb her, though. She was confident she could cope.

After checking on Max, who was asleep, Maggie made herself a cup of hot tea which she drank sitting in the kitchen waiting for Greg to return her call. Kevin, Josh, Wendy, and Kari burst into the duplex after school, clamoring for food. Maggie gave them apple slices smeared with peanut butter, and chocolate milk. Kristin arrived with two of the Jennifers. Still no call from Greg.

At a quarter past five the telephone rang at last and Maggie answered it eagerly, breathlessly. "Maggie, this is Paula," came a shaky, tear-filled voice. "I'm at the Community Hospital in southeast Washington and—"

"The hospital!" Maggie gasped. "Paula, what happened. Are you all right?"

"I'm okay, Maggie. I just have some cuts and bruises. There—there was a car accident and the police brought us here."

"Oh, my God!" Maggie sank into a chair.

"I couldn't reach my father so I called you." Paula's voice quavered. "Could you come and get me, Maggie?"

"Of course. But are you sure you're all right, Paula? You still haven't told me what happened."

"I'll tell you about it when you get here. I'm using the phone at the nurses' desk in the emergency room and I can't stay on long. Please come soon, Maggie."

"I'm leaving right now, Paula."

Maggie asked Mrs. Jenkins to stay with the children; she didn't think Max was well enough to be left in Kristin's care. It was still raining and traffic was maddeningly snarled, but Maggie managed to reach the hospital in just an hour. A nurse led her into the partitioned cubicle where Paula was sitting on the edge of the examining table. She was wearing her cheerleader's uniform: green and white pleated skirt, white crew-neck sweater emblazoned with a large green W, white socks, and sneakers. Her hair was pulled into two long pigtails and tied with green yarn. There was an angry lump above her left eyebrow and some scratches on her cheeks. She looked very young and very scared.

"Maggie!" Paula burst into tears at the sight of her. "Oh, Maggie, everything is awful! Todd has a concussion and a broken arm and the car is a wreck and his parents are furious!"

"What happened, Paula?" Maggie asked calmly. "Start from the beginning."

"Todd Terosky is my boyfriend," Paula said in a halting voice. "And he came to school to pick me up after the junior varsity football game. There wasn't anybody at home and so we decided to go for a ride."

In the pouring rain, Maggie thought. On the water-slick streets. Already she was questioning the young driver's judgment.

"We were riding around, just having fun and listening to the radio and this stupid fly was buzzing all around the car, driving us crazy." Paula paused and gulped. "We were trying to swat it and—and Todd sort of forgot to stop at a red light."

Maggie groaned. "Oh, Paula!"

"Don't be mad, Maggie." Paula began crying again. "Mr. Terosky went berserk when I told him. He started yelling at me and yelling at Todd and then Mrs. Terosky started."

"I can imagine." Maggie visualized the scene and grimaced. "I take it Todd's car was hit when he ran the red light?"

"By two cars, one on either side." Paula started to cry harder. "It was terrible, Maggie. I was so scared. And it happened so fast! I thought about my mother and I knew—I felt—" She buried her face in her hands and sobbed uncontrollably.

Maggie's heart went out to her. She put her arms around the weeping youngster and held her close, stroking her hair and whispering softly. Eventually Paula's tears subsided and Maggie talked with the harassed young intern on duty, signed the necessary release papers, and guided Paula out to her old Chevy in the hospital parking lot.

"Daddy is going to be furious," Paula said. Her voice was tremulous as she fastened her seat belt. "He didn't like the idea of me dating Todd in the first place."

"I know." Maggie steered the car onto the slick streets. "And I don't approve either, Paula. A four-teen-year-old has no business dating a high school boy with his own car. Honey, I don't want to upset you further, but today marks the end of your relationship with Todd Terosky."

Paula sniffled. "I sort of figured you'd say that."

Maggie was surprised by her tame reaction. Paula had obviously had a searing scare. She decided to press the advantage. "And there will be no more dates with older boys with cars, no more dates, period. Not until you're sixteen. Group parties and dances are fine for a girl your age. I think you should stick with your own age group, Paula."

"You sound like my girlfriends' mothers," Paula said with a trace of defiance. "Daddy lets me do any-thing I want."

"And it's scary to have all that freedom, isn't it, Paula?" Maggie asked gently. "I don't think you're as grown-up as your daddy thinks, are you, honey?" Paula began to cry again and cried the whole way home.

"Dr. Wilder called, Maggie," Mrs. Jenkins said when Maggie and Paula entered the duplex. "But I was busy with Max, so Kari answered the phone and took the message."

"Oh, dear." Maggie sighed. Kari's telephone messages tended to be somewhat garbled.

"Our new daddy got detoured at the hospital, Mommy," Kari said importantly.

Maggie smiled. "Detoured? Do you mean detained?"

Kari shrugged. "I don't know, but he's going to be late."

Mrs. Jenkins had fixed the children a soup-and-sandwich dinner and offered to do the same for Paula. Maggie was grateful for the offer of assistance. Max was feeling a little better, but was cranky and demanding. He wanted Maggie's exclusive attention and she decided to keep him with her for the night. And even if his fever broke before morning, he'd have to stay inside for at least twenty-four hours. She would have to report off work tomorrow and stay with him.

When Greg hadn't arrived by nine, Maggie sent Josh and Kevin to bed and put Wendy and Kari in the double bed in her room, figuring they might as well stay too. At ten she sent Kristin to bed and offered Paula the use of a nightgown and the sofa. Exhausted from her ordeal, Paula accepted the offer and was asleep within ten minutes.

"There isn't anywhere for *you* to sleep, Maggie," Mrs. Jenkins said. "And you missed your dinner too."

"The armchair in the living room is fairly comfortable. If I'm tired enough, I'll sleep," Maggie reassured her. "And I'll make myself a bologna and cheese sandwich." She thanked her neighbor, bid her good night, made the sandwich and ate it, and settled down to wait for Greg.

A car pulled to a stop in front of the duplex a few minutes before eleven. Maggie raced to the window and peered out. It wasn't the burgundy Cadillac or the tan station wagon. It was a sporty black Maserati and light was on inside the car. She could see Greg sitting on the passenger side. The driver was a woman.

Maggie walked outside to the car, heedless of the rain which had decreased to a light drizzle. Greg had already opened the car door, but hadn't yet climbed out. The woman in the driver's seat was talking animatedly to him in an obvious attempt to delay his departure. She was pretty, Maggie noted. Short, sleek blond hair, an engaging smile, well-dressed. And intent on charming Greg.

Maggie caught hold of the partially opened door

and swung it wide open. "Hi!" she said brightly, leaning inside the car.

The woman appeared slightly taken aback by the intrusion. Greg took a deep breath. "Maggie!" he said. He looked sick.

"Are you the baby-sitter?" the blonde asked incredulously.

"Among other things, yes." Maggie gave her an effervescent smile. "I was getting ready to put the bloodhounds on this man's trail."

Greg didn't meet her eyes. "I had car trouble, Maggie. I left the headlights on this morning and wore the battery down. It was totally dead when I came back to the parking lot tonight. Clare, here, Clare Priestly"—he inclined his head toward the blonde—"happened to be in the hospital lobby when I was phoning the auto club. She offered me a lift and I decided to take it instead of waiting around."

"It was terribly kind of you to drive Greg the whole way out here to Woodland, Clare," Maggie said sweetly. Nice try, Clare Priestly, she thought to herself, but this man is mine.

Perhaps Clare read the unspoken message in her eyes. "No trouble." The blonde shrugged. "I guess you don't want a rain check on that drink at my place, Greg?"

"Why, we'd be delighted, Clare," Maggie said, flashing her most charming smile. "Just give a call to confirm the date."

Greg coughed, shook his head, and got out of the car, mumbling a quick "Thanks for the ride."

Greg and Maggie walked in silence to the door of the duplex as Clare Priestly's black Maserati disappeared into the night. When they reached the doorstep, Greg grasped Maggie's shoulders and turned her around to face him. "Look," he said, "I know you don't believe me, but it's the truth, Maggie. I really did leave the headlights on and the car battery really was dead. Clare works in the hospital admitting office and she happened to come along and—"

"—offered you a ride and a drink at her place," Maggie finished for him. "And you accepted the ride and turned down the drink."

"Yes!" Greg's voice shook with vehemence. "I swear it's the truth, Maggie."

"I believe you," she said calmly. It was true. She'd suffered no pangs of jealousy at the sight of Greg with the blonde. Whatever Clare Priestly's motives in offering the ride, Maggie trusted Greg. He had asked her to marry him, to create a home with him. He wouldn't betray her. She knew that now. "After last night I—"

"After last night you don't give a damn? Believe me, I understand, Maggie. Last night should never have happened!" Greg said fiercely. "I spent all day regretting every minute of it, beginning with that imbecilic proposal!"

Maggie stood stock-still, immobilized by a stunning pain. She'd experienced a similar sensation once, when her older brother had accidentally hit her over the head with his baseball bat. Greg regretted his impulsive proposal; he'd spent the whole day regretting their night of love. She thought instantly of her children. How was she going to tell them that they weren't going to have a "new daddy" after all? And she thought of Josh and Wendy and little Max, who needed her maternal love and care, of Paula, who needed her guidance. They were all going to be hurt. But the children's pain couldn't come close to her own. How flat and lonely and painful her life would be without the man she loved! She would adjust—she would have to—but Maggie knew she would never be happy again.

"Maggie, can you forgive me?" Greg asked quietly. "I know that I've hurt you, but—"

"No!" She was suddenly, violently maddened with rage. She jerked herself out of his grip. "No, dammit, I can't forgive you! I won't!" She stormed inside, slamming the door behind her. Greg had turned her life upside down, had sparked her feelings and her dreams, only to walk away. He was breaking her heart and hurting the children, and he had the nerve to ask her forgiveness?

She didn't know where to go or what to do. The kitchen was the only room in the house without a sleeping child in it, so she went there and paced the floor like a madwoman. She was scarcely aware that she was crying. Tears were streaming down her cheeks and she didn't bother to wipe them away.

The doorbell rang, followed by a heavy knock on the door. She marched to the front door and flung it open, facing Greg on the doorstep. "If you dare to wake up these children . . ."

"Maggie, please! I don't have a car. I—"

"I'll call you a taxi!" She slammed the door in his face, leaving him standing on the doorstep in the drizzle. He looked so miserable. So tired and depressed and utterly alone.

And suddenly, abruptly, Maggie stopped crying. Something was wrong, terribly wrong. She leaned against the door, strangely calm now, and thought. Greg had been so insistent upon marrying her yesterday. He'd had a whole list of reasons, all of which remained unchanged. And they'd made love last night with a ferocity and a generosity of passion that simply couldn't be wiped out in the course of a day. She thought back to their prior misunderstandings, all stupid trifles that had been magnified by a lack of communication. She withdrew, he withdrew. They both suffered. Neither really knew the other yet. They were going to have to work hard at that. And pride and silence had no place in their relationship, not now or ever.

Before she could think of a reason not to, Maggie threw open the front door. "Come in here, Greg Wilder!" She grabbed his hands and tugged him toward her, pulling him inside. "We're going to talk."

"Maggie, I love you," he said swiftly. "I want to tell you that before either of us says another word."

She put her hands on her hips and faced him

with blazing green eyes. Her heart was pounding in her ears. "Do you or do you not want to marry me?"

"Maggie, I want to marry you more than anything in the world, but I've bungled so badly. I tried to rush you with a premature proposal, I selfishly demanded your emotional and physical surrender—"

"That I gave willingly," she cut in. "I love you, you idiot, but I have to agree that you certainly bungled badly. Telling me that you regretted proposing to me, that you were sorry you made love to me last night. Do you know how that sounded to me, Greg?"

He gazed into her luminous emerald eyes. "You were crying," he said softly, tracing a tear's path down her cheek with a gentle finger. "I'm sorry, love."

"I love you, Greg. I want to marry you and live with you and your kids and my kids and—and I want to have your baby."

"Oh, Maggie!" He pulled her into his arms and crushed her to him. "Darling, I think I'm dreaming. After this nightmare of a day . . . two emergency operations, my office schedule backed up four and a half hours, the car not starting and the ride home with Clare. I was so sure you'd be jealous and when you weren't, I was totally thrown. I thought you didn't care, that I'd lost you . . . I already felt guilty about last night and—" His arms tightened possessively. "Maggie, do you really love me?"

"I thought I made it obvious last night," she whispered, flushing a little at the memory of their abandoned passion.

"I knew I'd proven that I could make you surrender physically, but I was worried that I'd scared you away as well." Greg threaded his fingers through the auburn silkiness of her hair.

"Never, Greg." Maggie's mind swept over the events of the day: Max's ear infection, Paula's accident, and she thought of all the unpredictable and unexpected things that could occur in a family with seven children. Eight, she mentally corrected herself.

Greg's and her baby was already a reality in her mind. "I don't scare easily, my love."

They kissed, a long, deep kiss of mutual love and abiding passion. Eventually, reluctantly, they drew apart and wandered into the kitchen, their arms around each other. Maggie made hot chocolate and they sat down to drink it, with her comfortably settled in Greg's lap.

"Greg, all day long I've been thinking about the kids and my job," she began on a tentative note. "It will be an adjustment for all seven of them, living together with a new set of parents . . ."

"In a new house," Greg said.

"In a new house. And what happened with Max and Paula today made me think that maybe all the kids are going to need me at home for a while."

Greg tensed. "What happened with Max and Paula?"

Maggie told him. He was visibly shaken by the details of the accident and lambasted the careless teenage driver. "But I can understand why she went with him, why she didn't want to go home to that empty house," he added. "I think Paula at fourteen needs you to be at home after school as much as Max at four needs to be sprung from the child care center. And there are the five kids in between . . ."

"And the new baby, as yet unborn and unnamed," Maggie added, grinning.

"Oh, let's not forget the new baby, as yet unborn and unnamed." Greg chuckled, hugging her. "What do you want to do, honey?"

"I thought I'd quit my job and stay home with the kids. And if I wasn't working, I would have some time to take a course or two at one of the colleges or universities in Baltimore or D.C. Do you think it's impossible for a woman my age to get a degree, Greg?" she asked wistfully.

"I don't think anything is impossible for you, Maggie. You choose a college or university and start taking courses toward your degree. By the time the eighth Wilder child—the as yet unborn and unnamed one—is ready for school, I'll wager you'll have it."

"The tuition might be expensive," warned Maggie.

"We can afford it," Greg said in a magnanimous tone so like Paula's in the toy shop that Maggie laughed.

"Maggie." He gazed into her laughing eyes. "Mary Magdalene, I love you so."

"Don't call me that," she said lovingly. "And I love you, Greg Wilder."

Moments later there was an urgent tap at the back door. "What now?" Greg complained as Maggie hopped from his lap to answer it.

"Mrs. Jenkins!" she exclaimed in surprise.

Mrs. Jenkins entered the kitchen carrying her huge plastic knitting bag and a half-finished sweater. "I happened to notice Dr. Wilder's arrival and I happened to overhear your little spat. And then I noticed that there's a Cary Grant and Irene Dunne movie on the late show and I thought of your comfortable armchair. So here I am."

Greg stared at the woman as if she were daft, but Maggie smiled in dawning comprehension.

"Since I'll be here with the children," Mrs. Jenkins continued, "why don't the two of you spend the night someplace where you can be alone?" The elderly woman beamed at them. "May I suggest the Woodland Holiday Inn? Just five minutes down the road and my nephew is the desk clerk on duty."

"Why, Mrs. Jenkins, you're a romantic!" Maggie said, laughing. "And though it's a very generous offer, we couldn't possibly—"

"She's a regular fairy godmother," Greg interrupted. He stood up and wrapped an arm around Maggie's shoulders. "And we *can* and *are* going to accept her very generous offer. Get your toothbrush and your car keys, Maggie."

Mrs. Jenkins smiled her approval. "Of course, I am expecting an invitation to your wedding."

"Mrs. Jenkins, you've got it," Greg promised, and hurried Maggie to the door.

39,72f 10lf 161

THE EDITOR'S CORNER

Wonderful news! Alicia Condon, formerly at Silhouette/Harlequin, has joined our LOVESWEPT team as senior editor. Alicia is not only a delightful person, but also one of the most experienced editors in romance publishing. She started out six years ago at MacFadden where she edited such writers as Jayne (Castle) Krentz, Diana (Blaine) Palmer, and many others who've gone on to give us so much entertaining romantic fiction. She joined the Silhouette staff four years ago and was responsible for launching the Special Edition, Intimate Moments, and Desire lines. We are *so* glad to have Alicia with us to help continue the excellence of our LOVESWEPT publishing program!

Next month you can expect some more wonderful news from us—in the form of the four LOVESWEPT romances coming your way.

First we have another charming book by Joan Elliott Pickart, **FASCINATION,** LOVESWEPT #99. Heroine Robin Kent runs an employment service; hero Jeff Webster is a lawyer. They work in the same office complex, but only their gazes meet . . . across the courtyard. They grow more and more fascinated with one another and both do a little detective work to discover the other's identity. When they come face to face, their attraction zings! But have they got problems! She's a fast food junkie; he's a gourmet. She adores football; he detests the game. It's pure delight to accompany them along their rough path to love. And if there's ever been a niftier proposal of marriage, I'd like to know about it!

(continued)

Sara Orwig just keeps coming up with one marvelous, wonderfully different love story after another. **THE GOODIES CASE,** LOVESWEPT #100, is a heartwarming tale of a very lovely and very responsible young woman, Crystal, who's saddled with the most remarkably loony family! She's vowed to marry (soon) the dullest man she can find and never experience another crazy moment again in her life! Then she encounters Pug Moffitt (the encounter is hilarious!) and he is anything but dull! He is also determined to marry Crystal. This romance is delicious in more ways than one (how's that for titillating your interest?) and you won't want to miss it!

Marianne Shock made a smashing debut into romance publishing with **QUEEN'S DEFENSE,** LOVESWEPT #69. Now she is back with her second love story, **WORTHY OPPONENTS,** LOVESWEPT #101. Luke Hudson seemed to be a "mountain man," though a very polished one, and he made Kyla Trent's vacation into a thrilling time of discovery. Back in the "real" world of business, though, Kyla experienced an appalling twist of fate . . . one that she feared not even her "mountain man" could save her from. Vivid, intense, this is a splendid romance that I'm sure you will long remember.

We are always proud and pleased to be able to launch a brand new writer. And, so, we hope you will give a warm, warm welcome to our latest "find" —Eugenia Riley. **REMEMBER ME, LOVE?,** LOVESWEPT #102, is Eugenia's first short contemporary romance and it's a stunning first. Molly Buchanan is accompanying her aunt on a trip to L.A. that was a prize in a contest—or so the two ladies thought. Actually the trip is part of a bigger plot by Molly's ex-husband Nicky to win her back. There are wonderful secondary characters too in this delightful story . . . and a sensuality and tenderness that make **REMEMBER ME, LOVE?** a breathtaking romance.

As you know, we're delighted to get your letters about our LOVESWEPT romances. And we read them carefully and answer every one. Over the last several months, though, a number of you have forgotten to include your return address. If you haven't heard back from us, will you write again—this time including your address?

Warm regards,

Sincerely,

Carolyn Nichols

Carolyn Nichols
  Editor
LOVESWEPT
Bantam Books, Inc.
666 Fifth Avenue
New York, NY 10103

*A special excerpt of
the remarkable historical novel by
the author of* THE PROUD BREED
and THE TIGER'S WOMAN

WILD
SWAN
by Celeste De Blasis

RANE FALCONER WAS TIRED. The voyage to France had been a hard one with winds fickle and the revenue cutters much in evidence. They'd had to hide the goods in caves far down the coast the previous night rather than in the ones convenient to Clovelly. It meant more trouble retrieving them, by land or by sea. But right now, all Rane wanted to do was sleep. He usually felt this way after time on board with his father; Magnus was an exacting taskmaster, and Rane's eighteen-year-old body, tall and lanky, always seemed to crave more food and sleep than were allowed on the ship. He rearranged his plans to include eating anything his mother offered him before he fell into bed.

He had forgotten all about the distant cousin who was coming to stay with them. He had thought little of the matter at all except to consider that it would be nice for his mother to have a girl child to coddle; with three living sons, Gweneth declared herself more than content, but Rane knew she regretted the loss of two infant daughters, both dead at birth years apart and years ago.

He remembered the expected visitors as soon as he entered the house and heard his mother speaking to someone, but nothing eased his shock at his first sight of Alexandria Thaine.

It was like looking into an enchanted mirror that reflected his own image in female form. The planes of their faces were very similar, the dark hair of both framing the features, and green eyes met green eyes in stunned recognition. He heard the older woman gasp, but he and Alexandria remained silent for a long, wondering moment.

Now Alex understood why the various reactions—Seadon's, the villagers', Gweneth's—to her had been so strong. This resemblance went far beyond the similar family traits she shared with Gweneth.

And then Rane smiled at her, a warm welcoming smile that lighted his tired face. "Well, cousin, we would be hard pressed to deny kinship. I'm Rane, R-a-n-e, not R-a-i-n. Welcome to Clovelly." He had a sudden urge to hug her and reassure her as if she were even younger than her age; she looked so scared and somehow fragile, her eyes too big in her thin face and shadows making them seem even larger. She was holding herself stiffly upright, as if only pride were keeping her from bolting though she essayed a small attempt at a smile when he spelled his name.

The cold knot of misery that had gripped Alex since she had first heard of her exile to the West Country began to ease, thawed in some mysterious way by the mere presence of this tall young man. It was hard not to stare at him; it would take time to grow accustomed to this shared image. And she could not begin to understand why the features she found displeasing in herself should be so handsome in him. She had long known that her tall earthy looks had nothing in common with current fashion, her wild dark hair and green eyes so strong and vivid that she seemed out of place even in her own family. But the same in him formed a marvelous symmetry and seemed fitting for an inhabitant of this strange village by the sea.

The first days at Clovelly sped by so swiftly for Alex, she could scarcely keep track of where they began and where they ended; they were a rush of light upon light of new experiences with pauses of nightfall for sleep.

Virginia had seen the change even on the first day when Alexandria and Rane had returned to the house. The granddaughter she knew had reappeared—green eyes wide and alert with interest, mouth curved in a smile, and color beginning to show again in her cheeks.

She had come to her grandmother without hesitation, putting her arms around her and murmuring low, "I never should have doubted you! This is a wonderful, magical place! I shall be happy here, I know I shall!"

For Virginia, there was pain and pleasure both in Alexandria's acceptance. It was best for the child, but for the old woman, it meant weeks, months, a very long time without this being who so brightened her days. And she knew that Alexandria, already such a strange mix of young and old, would surely have passed beyond childhood completely by the next time they saw each other. But she had steeled herself against showing anything except approval and had known it would be better were she to leave the following week when she could get the coach from Bideford to Exeter and on to London. To tarry too long would only make it harder for both of them.

For Alex the farewell went as quickly as everything else seemed to in her new life. The pain and sudden longing for life in Gravesend, no matter how complicated, was sharp, but Gweneth was there to tell her that Seadon and Barbary woud pick her up on their way back tomorrow for a visit to the farm, and Rane was there, too, with more immediate plans, asking her if she would like to go aboard Magnus's ship, the *Lady Gwen*.

She had not yet been aboard the graceful ship, and the excitement of Rane's offer did much to banish the sorrow of her grandmother's departure.

Rane rowed her out to the *Lady Gwen*. Though the ship could be brought in close to the quay when tide and wind were right, Magnus preferred to keep her farther out for safety.

Alex had been on ships before, at Gravesend when she was quite small, and her father had taken her with him a few times when he was making sure goods he'd supplied were being properly delivered. The *Lady Gwen* was surely one of the trimmest and best kept vessels she had ever seen. Everything from wood to brass gleamed with care. But one thing puzzled her. Though the ship was obviously built for speed, the sleek lines cut down on the cargo space enough so that she noticed. However, she did not register the sly looks the two men on watch exchanged when she questioned Rane about it.

He barely restrained his start of surprise. He had discussed Alex's sharpness with his mother, and they both agreed that she was too quick-witted to be kept in ignorance forever. But Gweneth had insisted that it was better for the child to have time to adjust before she knew all of the Falconers' business, and Magnus had concurred. Still, even Rane had not expected she would question the limited cargo space of the ship. He had suppressed his unease and managed to answer calmly.

"We don't deal in large, bulky cargoes such as lime or clay. We carry more precious things, er ... china, housewares, some foodstuffs. We're paid more for transporting them, and we can do it swiftly with the *Lady Gwen*." He made the details purposefully vague and was relieved to see it made sense to Alex.

Though she found the ship interesting, she was even more enchanted by the view of Clovelly from out on the water. "I still find it difficult to believe what I'm seeing," she sighed. "It is surely the most beautiful village in all the world. You are very fortunate to live here."

"Indeed I am," Rane agreed gravely. "And now you live here, too." He meant a great deal more than an observation on life in the village. His mother had told him much about Alex's background, and he still could not credit that parents should be so careless with such an appealing child. She made him feel much older than his eighteen years and very protective.

"You don't have to tell me, but if you'd ever like to talk about the trouble at your home, I can listen," he offered gently and was instantly sorry he had.

She stiffened and looked so hurt and lost, he wanted to comfort her as if she were truly a small child, but instead, he listened intently as she told him the story of what she had done. The words tumbled out very quickly, the condemned confessing right before the execution.

"Is that really what happened?" he asked, his voice strangled.

"Yes, but my mother and my sister don't like me very well in any case, so that made it worse."

Despite his efforts to prevent it, Rane was laughing. He knew it was important and tragic to her, but the image of this grave-faced child creating such havoc for her dull family amused him mightily.

"Oh, Alex, don't you see how foolish they all were?" he gasped. "If this Carrington were any kind of man and your sister any kind of woman, nothing you could have said would have made the slightest difference. It's just our good luck that your mother and sister are so hideously stupid and the rest of the lot so cowardly." He stopped suddenly, appalled by what he had said.

But her reaction was again unexpected. "Not my grandmother," she protested solemnly, and then she was laughing, too, suddenly seeing her mother and sister as red-faced, ranting puppets, too small and far away to harm her more. And Rane had called her "Alex" as if they'd been friends for a long time, his voice warm; it gave her an identity beyond the odd relative left to be cared for.

She saw the truth of Rane's contention—if Florence and St. John really cared for each other, neither she nor anyone else would be able to keep them from each other. She thought of Gweneth and Magnus and doubted that any power on earth could have kept them apart. Peace and joy flooded through her; she felt as if she had come home.

In the days that followed, her sense of newness was replaced by a feeling that she had always lived here, and gradually she began to play an active role in Falconer family life, finding her skills appreciated, her help eagerly accepted when she offered it. She loved the farm from the first day she saw it and proved herself useful in milking the cow, collecting eggs from the fowl, and other chores long since familiar because of time spent on Virginia's land.

In Clovelly she was soon helping Gweneth prepare the meals, and more, she was trusted to treat minor ailments. Magnus was her first patient when he suffered a nasty gash on his forearm. At Gweneth's command, he kept his skepticism to himself and allowed Alex to clean and dress the cut. When he found how much she had eased the discomfort and saw how well the wound healed, he could not have been more generous in his praise had she been one of his own children.

But as much as she was warmed by the kindness of the rest of the family, best of all for Alex were the hours spent with Rane. He took her fishing, and she was soon adept at repairing nets and lines. She applied holystone to the decks of the *Lady Gwen* with a will and polished brass fittings until they shone as brightly as Magnus liked. If Rane were helping out on the farm, she was glad to do any task as long as she was allowed to be with him.

Alex sensed a restlessness in Rane stronger than that in the other men. He was seldom still, but when he was, there was often a faraway look in his eyes, as if he were contemplating horizons he had not yet seen. His need for action was to her advantage because it led to their explorations of the countryside, on foot or sometimes on the ponies. And even in the bitter cold with a knife-edged wind blowing salt spray, one of Rane's favorite haunts was Hartland Point, a jutting red-hued cliff over the sea. Jagged rocks waited some three hundred and fifty feet below to rake the fragile hulls of unwary ships. Alex did not question why it was so, but in spite of the bleakness of the place, she felt exhilarated and washed clean when she came to the Point, and she knew Rane felt the same. Sometimes they would sit for a long time, hunkered down against the cold, sometimes talking lazily, sometimes silent because they could not compete with the roar of the wind and the sea. Even when the elements were wild, here Rane was often at his most peaceful.

On clear days, they could see Lundy, the Norse name meaning "Isle of Puffins," a place rich in legend. It was said that a member of Parliament from Barnstaple had transported convicts there instead of to Virginia in America where they were legally bound. He had used them as slaves to hack out a cave for storing smuggled goods until his malfeasance was discovered and he was arrested.

Alex shivered at the thought of being a prisoner there. "To be confined to so small a piece of land, I would go mad!"

Rane nodded, relieved that the fact of the M.P.'s business seemed to be of no importance to her compared to the lot of his victims. "I, too. There is so much of the world to see!"

"If you marry Mary Forthy, she'll understand that. She might even sail with you, being Clovelly born. But then, I suppose the same could be said of the widow from Buck's Mills or any other woman who lives so close to ships and the sea, born here or not."

For a moment, Rane was speechless. It hadn't occurred to him that Alex was aware of his love life, but he saw now that she could scarcely be in ignorance of it. His brothers teased him unmercifully about the accommodating woman at Buck's Mills, and Mary Forthy, a comely blond of seventeen, was less than subtle in her pursuit of him. The widow, ten years older than he, had long since lost her status as an amateur and was not a candidate for marriage, and would undoubtedly refuse even were she asked. She was clean, discreet, and skilled, but the favors, physical and otherwise, of one man would never satisfy her. Local wags had it that her husband, years older than she, had died of overwork without leaving the house. Mary, on the other hand, was exactly what most men looked for in a wife. She was pretty, capable of running a household smoothly, and bright enough though not overly educated. But the idea of spending his life with her gave Rane exactly the same feeling he got when he contemplated being a prisoner on Lundy. Mary's adoration was more of an embarrassment than a compliment, and Rane found it very convenient to have Alex beside him as she tended to serve as a buffer against Mary's attentions.

"Mary is a sweet lass, but I haven't any plans in that direction, so please don't make any for me. And as for the widow, well, she is not the sort of woman you ought to be thinking about at all," he added.

Alex blushed, remembering the painted women in London and those she had seen in Gravesend, but she was relieved. She, too, thought Mary a nice enough person, but not good enough for Rane. She hoped he would find someone more like the women his brothers had married. Suddenly she was up and running away from the Point, calling that she would beat him to the ponies.

She just managed to do it because of her head start, and they rode companionably back toward the farm, stopping only to watch a flight of swans pass overhead. These were not the common Mute swans nor yet the Whooper swans, but rather smaller foreigners. Their wing beats did not sing as did the Mute's; they passed over in nearly silent grace, the soft *hoo-hoo-hoo* of their voices sounding like nothing more than the wind sighing. And they flew in what seemed a random pattern rather than in the trailing chevron of Whooper swans. They were not native to Britian, nesting instead in more northeasterly countries, some said as far away as Russia, and their coming was an indication of hard weather elsewhere.

"I love them all," Alex said reverently. "These with their soft music when they're feeding, Whooper swans with their loud chorus, and the Mute swans, the royal birds who act as if they own the Thames and every other river and pond in England and are surely not mute! I remember the first time I heard one of them hiss. I was very small, and it frightened me properly. My grandmother explained that it was just warning me not to come too close, and that seemed reasonable once I'd thought about it."

They watched the birds out of sight, sharing their mutual love and knowledge of the wild things. Many were not even aware that these frosty white birds were swans, thinking instead they were geese and thus missing the essential mystery of the birds who wandered so far. Knowing exactly what things were was a way of getting closer to the earth, a skill long taught to Alex by her grandmother and to Rane by both of his parents.

"Perhaps they are swan maidens with fine gold chains around their necks," Rane murmured, whimsy as much a part of his nature as the more rational aspects. "When they settle on secret ponds and lakes, they take off their feather cloaks and are beautiful women, eternally young. That's who I'll wed, one of the swan maidens."

Alex knew the old legend as well as he. "You'll have to take care. Remember that if you do not hide the cloak, she will fly away."

Though he did not remember it, that night Rane dreamed he captured a swan whose feather cloak fell away to reveal not Mary Forthy nor the Buck's Mills' widow, but Alexandria. In his dream she was older, her body more curved, but still she was Alex.

*   *   *

Sweeping from England's West Country in the years of the Napoleonic Wars when smuggling flourished and life was led dangerously, to the beauty of Maryland horse country—a golden land already shadowed by slavery and soon to be ravaged by war—here is a novel richly spun of authentically detailed history and sumptuous romance, the story of a woman's life and the generations of two families interwoven by fortune and fate, told as it could only be by the bestselling author of THE PROUD BREED.

Don't miss WILD SWAN,
available in paperback July 1, 1985,
from Bantam Books.

A Stirring Novel of Destinies
Bound by Unquenchable Passion

SUNSET EMBRACE

by Sandra Brown

Fate threw Lydia Russell and Ross Coleman, two untamed outcasts, together on a Texas-bound wagon train. On that wild road, they fought the breathtaking desire blazing between them, while the shadows of their enemies grew longer. As the train rolled west, danger drew ever closer, until a showdown with their pursuers was inevitable. Before it was over, Lydia and Ross would face death . . . the truth about each other . . . and the astonishing strength of·their love.

Buy SUNSET EMBRACE, on sale January 15, 1985 wherever Bantam paperbacks are sold, or use the handy coupon below for ordering:

The stunning novel of a glittering dream come true ...

PROMISES
&
LIES

by Susanne Jaffe

Valerie Cardell—a shy girl in a small midwest town. Hers was a Cinderella story in search of a happy ending—an ending she found by defying her family to marry David Kinnelon, society's most eligible, most desirable bachelor. She became a ravishing New York socialite and reveled in a glittering world of dreams come true.

But now that dream is threatened by her own family—who would bring the Kinnelon empire crashing down, whose blind hatred could destroy Valerie's world ... forever.

Don't miss PROMISES & LIES, coming in March 1985 from Bantam Books, or use this handy coupon for ordering:

#1 HEAVEN'S PRICE
By Sandra Brown
Blair Simpson had enclosed herself in the fortress of her dancing, but Sean Garrett was determined to love her anyway. In his arms she came to understand the emotions behind her dancing. But could she afford the high price of love?

#2 SURRENDER
By Helen Mittermeyer
Derry had been pirated from the church by her ex-husband, from under the nose of the man she was to marry. She remembered every detail that had driven them apart—and the passion that had drawn her to him. The unresolved problems between them grew . . . but their desire swept them toward surrender.

#3 THE JOINING STONE
By Noelle Berry McCue
Anger and desire warred within her, but Tara Burns was determined not to let Damon Mallory know her feelings. When he'd walked out of their marriage, she'd been hurt. Damon had violated a sacred trust, yet her passion for him was as breathtaking as the Grand Canyon.

#4 SILVER MIRACLES
By Fayrene Preston
Silver-haired Chase Colfax stood in the Texas moonlight, then took Trinity Ann Warrenton into his arms. Overcome by her own needs, yet determined to have him on her own terms, she struggled to keep from losing herself in his passion.

#5 MATCHING WITS
By Carla Neggers
From the moment they met, Ryan Davis tried to outmaneuver Abigail Lawrence. She'd met her match in the Back Bay businessman. And Ryan knew the Boston lawyer was more woman than any he'd ever encountered. Only if they vanquished their need to best the other could their love triumph.

#6 A LOVE FOR ALL TIME
By Dorothy Garlock
A car crash had left its

marks on Casey Farrow's beauty. So what were Dan Murdock's motives for pursuing her? Guilt? Pity? Casey had to choose. She could live with doubt and fear . . . or learn a lesson in love.

#7 A TRYST WITH MR. LINCOLN?
By Billie Green
When Jiggs O'Malley awakened in a strange hotel room, all she saw were the laughing eyes of stranger Matt Brady . . . all she heard were his teasing taunts about their "night together" . . . and all she remembered was nothing! They evaded the passions that intoxicated them until . . . there was nowhere to flee but into each other's arms.

#8 TEMPTATION'S STING
By Helen Conrad
Taylor Winfield likened Rachel Davidson to a Conus shell, contradictory and impenetrable. Rachel battled for independence, torn by her need for Taylor's embraces and her impassioned desire to be her own woman. Could they both succumb to the temptation of the tropical paradise and still be true to their hearts?

#9 DECEMBER 32nd . . . AND ALWAYS
By Marie Michael
Blaise Hamilton made her feel like the most desirable woman on earth. Pat opened herself to emotions she'd thought buried with her late husband. Together they were unbeatable as they worked to build the jet of her late husband's dreams. Time seemed to be running out and yet—would ALWAYS be long enough?

#10 HARD DRIVIN' MAN
By Nancy Carlson
Sabrina sensed Jacy in hot pursuit, as she maneuvered her truck around the racetrack, and recalled his arms clasping her to him. Was he only using her feelings so he could take over her trucking company? Their passion knew no limits as they raced full speed toward love.

LOVESWEPT

*Love Stories you'll never forget
by authors you'll always remember*

☐	21603	**Heaven's Price #1** Sandra Brown	$1.95
☐	21604	**Surrender #2** Helen Mittermeyer	$1.95
☐	21600	**The Joining Stone #3** Noelle Berry McCue	$1.95
☐	21601	**Silver Miracles #4** Fayrene Preston	$1.95
☐	21605	**Matching Wits #5** Carla Neggers	$1.95
☐	21606	**A Love for All Time #6** Dorothy Garlock	$1.95
☐	21609	**Hard Drivin' Man #10** Nancy Carlson	$1.95
☐	21611	**Hunter's Payne #12** Joan J. Domning	$1.95
☐	21618	**Tiger Lady #13** Joan Domning	$1.95
☐	21613	**Stormy Vows #14** Iris Johansen	$1.95
☐	21614	**Brief Delight #15** Helen Mittermeyer	$1.95
☐	21616	**A Very Reluctant Knight #16** Billie Green	$1.95
☐	21617	**Tempest at Sea #17** Iris Johansen	$1.95
☐	21619	**Autumn Flames #18** Sara Orwig	$1.95
☐	21620	**Pfarr Lake Affair #19** Joan Domning	$1.95
☐	21621	**Heart on a String #20** Carla Neggars	$1.95
☐	21622	**The Seduction of Jason #21** Fayrene Preston	$1.95
☐	21623	**Breakfast in Bed #22** Sandra Brown	$1.95
☐	21624	**Taking Savannah #23** Becky Combs	$1.95
☐	21625	**The Reluctant Lark #24** Iris Johansen	$1.95

Prices and availability subject to change without notice.

Buy them at your local bookstore or use this handy coupon for ordering:

Bantam Books, Inc., Dept. SW, 414 East Golf Road, Des Plaines,
Ill. 60016

Please send me the books I have checked above. I am enclosing $_____
(please add $1.25 to cover postage and handling). Send check or money order
—no cash or C.O.D.'s please.

Mr/Mrs/Miss_____

Address_____

City_____State/Zip_____

SW—6/85
Please allow four to six weeks for delivery. This offer expires 12/85.

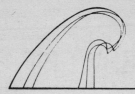

LOVESWEPT

Love Stories you'll never forget by authors you'll always remember